"Good God! He didn't try to force himself on you!"

I opened my lips to object, and was suddenly wrapped in a crushing embrace that took the breath out of me. Paton's lips moved in a frenzy of nibbling kisses over my ears and eyes and lips. "Poor Emma! And here I have been thinking ill of you. I should be beaten."

I was speechless at this unexpected outpouring. I felt hot tears gathering in my eyes. It was all so strange and surprising and lovely to be loved. I felt a smile tremble on my lips. Before I said anything, Paton lowered his head and firmed my quivering lips with his. It was like a spark to tinder. . . .

ROMANTIC REBEL

Joan Smith

FAWCETT CREST • NEW YORK

A Fawcett Crest Book
Published by Ballantine Books
Copyright © 1991 by Joan Smith

Library of Congress Catalog Card Number: 90-93478

ISBN 0-449-21660-8

Manufactured in the United States of America

First Edition: February 1991

Chapter One

My father was reading *Émile* shortly before his death. I have no opinion of that rabble-rousing author, Rousseau, who decreed, among other absurdities, that women should be educated to serve and please men. My blood boils at the very memory of those infamous lines. That pernicious doctrine is partly responsible for the position I now find myself in. Nesbitt Hall was entailed on Cousin Geoffrey, so Rousseau is not responsible for his taking over my home when Papa died, but I might at least have been left money enough to make me independent. Instead of that, I am at the mercy of Geoffrey. He and my father concurred absolutely with the Frenchman, who ordered that "women have, or ought to have, but little liberty." Between the pair of them, they schemed to curtail my liberty to either marrying Geoffrey or being destitute.

I chose the latter. One of the perquisites Rousseau bestowed on gentlemen was that they should follow their instinct. I took the privilege for my own. And without any monetary help from the Ogre (Geoffrey), I now enjoy a sort of precarious independence. Thank you, Rousseau. It was fury with you that made me take up pen and spew out all the poison that was choking me. God bless you, Mr. Pepper, for accepting my essay and giving me a contract to publish it in your magazine, and paying me what I consider a quite inordinate sum for the privilege (*The Ladies' Journal*, October 1, 1817, entitled "A Daughter's Dilemma," by an Anonymous Gentlewoman, if you wish to have a glance at it).

The "anonymous" is not due to shame for my outspoken tirade against injustice. I would proudly scream Emma Nesbitt in letters ten feet high if I had my way. I only withheld my name for the family's sake. My Scotch aunts Theodora and Ariadne are getting on in years. They are perfect models of Rousseau's ideal ladies, and as they are both as rich as Croesus, my instinct bade me not to offend them by any impropriety. The appearance of a lady's name in print for any other reason than to announce her birth, marriage, or death would be considered extremely questionable by them. By hook or by crook, I'm determined to be rich yet, even if it means hoodwinking my aunts.

Mr. Pepper kindly mentioned in his letter that he would be most interested to see any other essays I had on hand. The words "always delighted to discover a new writing talent" and "would be honored if you would call on me to discuss further articles next time you are in Bath" gave impetus to my departure. I had sent my article to a London publishing firm as well, not really expecting to hear from them. Actually I did receive a rejection two days later, but by then I was too euphoric to care. Bath was more my style than wicked London. And of course it was the check for five guineas that made my going to Bath possible.

My chaperone, a sharp-tongued, repressed spinster cousin named Annie Potter, tried to stop me. "Take off to Bath with five guineas in your pocket? You're mad, my girl. It cannot be done."

"Can it not? The arrangements have already been made. I have booked seats on the mail coach and room at a hotel in Bath for two, but if you are not interested in accompanying me, then I shall go alone." I am not so harebrained as this speech would suggest. By means of those little economies practiced by every housekeeper since Eve, I had a couple of hundred pounds put away. My aunts usually gave me money for my birthday as well.

After a few bouts with Annie, she agreed to accompany me on what she chose to call a visit, but I had no notion of ever returning, except possibly to see old friends and gloat over Geoffrey after I am famous.

I informed Cousin Geoffrey over dinner a few nights later of my departure. He asked where I was going but did not inquire when, or indeed if I ever meant to return, and I did not volunteer the information.

"I must return to Iverton to wind up a few business details," he said. "I am leaving tomorrow morning, and shall be gone three days. I hope you have a pleasant journey, Emma."

"You also," I replied woodenly. The outward shell of civility was maintained throughout my cousin's takeover, doing considerable damage to my internal organs.

The unworthy thought popped into my head that he had invented this trip to his old home on the spot to deny me the use of the carriage. It made not a ha'penny's difference to me. In fact, it turned out for the best. With Geoffrey out of the house, I had more freedom for my packing, and took three trunks with me, leaving behind only my mourning gowns.

"You're never wearing a blue gown, and your poor papa hardly cold in his grave!" Annie exclaimed when I dressed on the fateful morning.

You'd think it was Joseph's coat of many colors to hear her rave. My decent navy gown was just a step livelier than mourning. "Papa was cold before Death got its hands on him. I will not indulge in the hypocrisy of mourning a man who treated me so abominably. If I had a scarlet gown, I'd dance through the streets in it before leaving!"

"Oh, Missie!" she said, highly distraught. "Your father did not mean any harm. He was just afraid some fortune hunter would rob you of the money. You know you were always headstrong, darting off without thinking, just like this visit."

"He never liked me, Annie. He pushed me off to school every chance he got, and treated me like a stranger when I was home. If it weren't for you, I would have been reared by servants. I cannot mourn for him after that will. You know in your heart I am right, even if I offend the proprieties."

She looked at me aslant from her sharp green eyes and drew a deep sigh. "You have seemed happier since receiving Pepper's letter. At least you don't strut about with your jaw clamped all hard and square, looking ready to kill someone. I should like

4

to know what you wrote, that he gave you five guineas for it."

"I wrote the truth," I said, jaw once again assuming an angular appearance. "That women in England are treated no better than children. Good God, I am two years older than Cousin Geoffrey, and ten times as clever, yet the law handed over to him my ancestral home, and Papa gave him my fortune. The amazing thing is that Mr. Pepper chose to publish it. He must be a very daring gentleman. I look forward to meeting him."

Annie wore enough crape for both of us. I talked her into leaving off the face veil for the trip, but she was in black from head to toe.

As the coach rattled through the downs of Devon into the lusher countryside of Somerset, I enjoyed a daydream of my brilliant future. Until the day my father's will was read, I never entertained much interest in how we ladies are treated by society. One accepts customs, however bizarre they prove upon examination to be. I felt an occasional prick of annoyance at having to await some footman's pleasure before I could drive into town, perhaps. From time to time interesting gentlemen visited the neighborhood, and it always seemed the more interesting they were, the louder Papa shouted that I would not be permitted to meet them. On those few occasions, I rather wished I had a gentleman's freedom, but for the most part, I enjoyed being Miss Nesbitt. It seemed to me the grosser iniquities were visited on the poor. Now I would have a taste of that as well.

My reading was largely limited to novels, the more gothic the better. Had it not been for Cousin Geoffrey's oblique mention of Rousseau's part in my father's will, I doubt I would have struggled through a novel written all in French. But reading that subversive thing on top of the misfortune that had befallen me, I came to a sudden realization that I had been treated like a child all my life. Dashing off my infamous essay took care of my fit of pique. My future writings would take a quite different course. I would become the next Mrs. Radcliffe. My father had provided me with a plot: I the hapless heroine, Cousin Geoffrey the villain, and the hero . . .

Like any lovelorn romantical lady, I had been busy turning my savior, Mr. Pepper, into Prince Charming. He would miraculously rescue me from the abyss of my woes. My fortune would be restored, with a husband thrown in for good measure. Mr. Pepper would be tall, elegantly lean, and dark of complexion. Oh, it was a lovely trip to Bath, interrupted only by the invariably complaining statements of Annie Potter.

"Garlic," she whispered in my ear when a new patron entered the coach at Glastonbury. If he smelled of garlic, the aroma was overriden by a not unpleasing scent of Steeke's Lavender Water.

"I don't see why the roads should be so rutted in the autumn," she grouched on another occasion, when we hit a minor bump.

The man smelling of garlic was so unwise as to volunteer a word. "You think this is bad. I've just been out west, toward Cornwall. Terrible what they call a road in the West."

Annie snapped her eyes at him, showed him her back, and said in a quite loud voice, "Impertinence!"

My daydream continued after this little contretemps. We had left Milverton on the morning coach. We arrived at Bath as twilight was falling. Everything was fine until the coach arrived, and we were put down in a bustling, cobbled coaching yard, with people shouting at the top of their lungs all about us. I looked at Annie, she looked at me with a wild eye, and I knew she was shaking in her shagreen slippers. I felt quite out of my depths, and was happy it was not London that had accepted my essay.

Lacking a servant, we should be demanding our own trunks and locating a hackney to take us to the hotel. We were such greenheads, and there was such confusion, all we could do was stare. To make oneself heard over the din was impossible, unless one's voice had been trained at an auctioneer's school. The so-called gentlemen jostled us aside and had their luggage put down. They managed to get hold of all the hackneys, and in a short space of time Annie and I were the only remaining passengers, standing alone in the great cobbled yard, with our trunks sitting on the ground beside us.

"This is a fine how-do-you-do," she said, pinning me with an accusing eye.

Lady Luck was with me. At that moment a late-arriving hackney drove into the yard. In a trice, our trunks were stored above and we were inside, driving to the Pelican Inn, where the late writer, Doctor Samuel Johnson, used to stay when he was in Bath. Papa stayed there once when he came to take the waters. Of course, he had not brought me with him, but he said it was centrally located and genteel without charging a fortune.

We were very well pleased with our rooms. It was my intention to go in search of regular lodgings the

7

very next day, but for this one night we had each our own room. And soon we would have an apartment, paid for by my pen.

With evening settling in, we had no intention of venturing into the town before morning. Fatigue from travel, if not propriety, would keep us indoors. After dinner in our rooms I wrote a note to Mr. Pepper, to be delivered to his publishing house the next morning at nine. In it I requested an interview at his earliest convenience. This done, I was free to spend my time deciding what outfit would make the grandest impression on him. I put my faith in the old adage that first impressions are lasting, and meant to cut a dash.

Annie finally accepted that I could not wear black when every black stitch I owned was still at Nesbitt Hall. She consoled herself that no one in Bath would know of the recent death, and agreed with me that my navy serge pelisse was not unhandsome. With it I wore my matching bonnet, trimmed with the eye of peacock feathers, which added a certain je ne sais quoi. If pushed to give a translation, "elegant" would do.

We studied the Rooms to Let columns of the journal for the remainder of the evening, consulting our map and circling those that were within easy walking distance of the center of town. At ten o'clock Annie declared she was so tired even her hair ached, and went to bed. I closed the intervening door and prowled my room awhile, too restless to settle down.

Eventually I put on my nightdress and went to the mirror to brush out my hair. It was rather a dingy mirror, and ill lit, which suited me just fine at that hour of the night. I didn't want too clear an image of

8

the lady staring back at me. I knew well enough she was no longer in the first blush of youth. Twenty-seven, and looked every month of it. But in the kindly shadows of night, she did not appear unattractive.

The light from behind glowed like copper through my hair as I brushed it. It was long, wavy, and quite luxurious in texture. My face looked uncommonly pale, but I put it down to fatigue. Pallor emphasized the size and darkness of my green eyes. They looked like dark emeralds, but in daylight would be revealed as closer to the inferior peridot. My nose was straight, and my jaw firm. Too firm. How the anger lingered over the inequity of that will! I consciously relaxed it, forcing my lips to curve upward. There, that was better.

At a sturdy five feet and six inches, I had no hope of appearing femininely fragile, but at least I no longer looked angry. The embers of resentment were there, burning inside, but I did not want to look like a harpy to the inhabitants of this new world I was entering, especially to Mr. Pepper.

The day I received Mr. Pepper's letter, I began keeping a sort of combination diary and Common Book, in which I jotted down a few thoughts each night before retiring. So little written by a female pen has been recorded for history. Many years hence, when my bones had turned to dust, some scholar might want these insights into the mind of an enlightened lady of the early nineteenth century. I sat with pen poised, waiting for the important images of the day to rise to the surface.

I wrote: I have cut the cord tying me to Nesbitt Hall and a life of docile servitude to Geoffrey Nesbitt. The beginning of a new life. Henceforth, I am a free agent. I shall do no man's bidding. Point to ponder—why has it taken me so long? We are all victims of habit and that tired old tyrant, Tradition.

It was a short entry, but to the point. I was tired and went to bed.

Chapter Two

I AWOKE IN the morning to the unwelcome sight and sound of rain pelting against the windowpane. It seemed an inauspicious beginning to my new life. Superstition, however, is for the ignorant, and I considered only the practicalities involved. Annie and I must put off looking for rooms till the rain let up. My letter to Mr. Pepper could certainly be delivered, rain or no. And I trust he was eager enough to see me that he would send a reply by return messenger.

I went to Annie's room, cheerfully calling, "Good morning."

She greeted me with a surly look and a waspish "What's good about it? I've been up for hours. How on earth does a body get a cup of tea in this place?"

"Ring for one next time, goose! I am ready for breakfast. Shall we go below?"

We descended in state to the lobby, where half a dozen patrons examined us as if they had never seen two provincial ladies before. I heard one young lad, not older than five or six, whisper to his mama, "Isn't she pretty?" and honored him with a smile. His nanny glared at me as though I were a lightskirt, but I think it was my elegant bonnet that incurred her wrath. She was done up in oxidated bombazine and a plain black round bonnet herself.

We hired a private parlor, and over breakfast we drew out our well-worn newspaper and settled on three sets of rooms to examine as soon as the rain let up. As if eager to see us move on, it stopped by the time we left the parlor.

"The streets will be sopping wet," Annie cautioned.

"We can hardly trail around town in clogs. Wear your second-best slippers. I intend to."

I had seen Bath twice before on visits to my aunts in Scotland, but it never looked so beautiful to me as it did that morning, all washed and shining in the sunlight. I think Bath must be one of the loveliest cities in England. It is shaped like a bowl, of which we stood at the bottom, gazing up at the steep tiers of the downs, with lovely Palladian buildings nestling amongst the trees. The peaceful Avon circles it all like a ribbon on a gown. It immediately flashed into my head that a description of Bath would make an interesting article for *The Ladies' Journal*.

This same lovely geography makes walking deuced difficult, of course, but it was not our intention to do much climbing up the steep hills. The three marks on our map were centrally located. Until I could afford to set up a carriage, we must reside close to the city's creature comforts. After a dismal hour of looking at one set of rooms after another, each dingier and more expensive and offering less in the way of amenities than the last, we agreed we

12

must give in and look up the hill, a little farther away from the Roman Baths.

"But first we shall visit the Pump Room," I decided. "It is all the go, Annie. A sort of meeting place, like High Street at home, only enclosed."

"Don't expect me to drink those stinking waters, for I shan't."

"I'm sure they serve tea, if you are determined not to look after your health."

"There's nothing amiss with my health. It's my head I should have looked at, letting you drag me here."

Annie had her tea, and I rather wished I had followed her example. The water tasted wretched. I cannot believe anything so vile can possibly do a body any good. But the scenery at least was unexceptionable. The classical architecture of the Pump Room is one of the sights of Bath, along with the Cathedral and the Municipal Building. It was very handsome inside, with the fountain and grand Tompion clock watching over all as it ticked away the seconds of our lives. A lively array of visitors promenaded all around, stopping to chat to friends.

After tea we joined the promenade, and received our fair share of quizzing by the gentlemen. It was clear at a glance we were not in London. The costumes were elegant enough, but of a noticeably provincial cut. My own blue ensemble was as good as anything in the room. Papa was never clutch-fisted when alive, which made his will all the harder to comprehend.

When we had had our fill of the promenade, Annie said what had to be said. "Shall we have another look at the advertisements, and see what other rooms are available?"

"Yes, but let us go back to the hotel for lunch first. Perhaps Mr. Pepper has replied to my note."

There was a letter awaiting me, urging me to go to see Mr. Pepper at once. This buoyed my spirits remarkably. I waited only to eat, brush my hair, and change into my best slippers, for the streets were quite dry by this time, and I was eager to make a grand appearance. Annie insisted I could not visit a gentleman alone, even if it was business, and as Bath was rather old-fashioned, I agreed.

I was glad she was with me when the cab headed across the bridge to the wrong side of Bath. I pulled the check string and stuck my head out the window. "There must be some mistake!" I exclaimed. "The publishing house cannot be here. It looks like a farming area." The rough road was filled with cattle, and such buildings as there were differed widely from the Palladian beauty of Bath.

"Temple Back is yonder, north of the Cattle Market," he replied. I had no recourse but to let him proceed, slowly, with the cattle taking precedence. Mr. Pepper's letter said Temple Back.

After a long, jolting, expensive drive, we were deposited at the door of a weather-beaten old barn of a place. I could scarcely believe my eyes when I saw a small placard proclaiming Pepper Publishing Company. I felt I ought to give back the five guineas and let Mr. Pepper buy a gallon of paint. In my heart I knew no hero dwelt within those walls.

The exterior alerted me not to expect anything in the way of grandeur, or even much of respectability, inside. It was a dusty, rambling, ramshackle building, with a flock of dirty urchins darting about the halls. One door stood open, and a little white-haired gnome of a man in spectacles, wearing a blue jacket with the elbows worn shiny, peered out.

"You'd be Miss Nesbitt, then?" he enquired in an accent from the east side of London.

"Yes, I'm looking for Mr. Pepper."

"You've found him. Come in, come in. Don't mind the dirt."

With sinking heart I entered his squalid office, Annie clutching my elbow. We stared around with wide eyes, as if we were at a raree-show. He had a battered old desk, piled high with papers, a chair behind it, and another chair in front. The walls were grimed with age and dust. No picture enlivened the vast expanse of grayish-yellow paint. There were not only rolls of dust, but actually pebbles on the carpet, along with a wizened rind of orange and some strange black pellets, which I originally took for the droppings of a rabbit, but eventually discovered to come from his pipe.

"Sit yourselves down," he offered, and wheeled his own chair out for Annie. I sat in the other, and very nearly fell off. One leg was short, but he jammed a book under it and it stopped jiggling. Mr. Pepper, my hero, leaned against the desk and smiled, while examining me closely.

"I'd a notion you'd be a deal older, and uglier," he said.

All I could think of to reply was "Oh." He certainly excelled my expectations on both counts. I presented Annie, who was rigid with disapproval.

"Not that it matters," he assured me. "You have the gift, and that's all I'm after. A fine, impassioned piece of prose you sent me, Miss Nesbitt. I'm ready to take anything else of the sort you have to offer."

This, at least, was what I had hoped to hear, and I began to recover. "I brought a few things with me." I opened my folio and handed him the two essays residing there. One was on the arrival of autumn in the country, with florid descriptions of changing colors and some analogy to life's passage. The other was a brief history and description of the old Perpendicular Church in Milverton, which has some fine wood carvings.

He glanced at them briefly and looked at me, bewildered. "But these are pap," he said simply.

"What do you mean? They are elegant descriptions of . . ."

"This isn't the sort of thing I publish at all, Miss Nesbitt. Your other piece, now, that was more like it. There are half a dozen magazines putting out this sort of drivel. I print a few of them. Not publish, mind, but print. This building is an old printer's workshop. I began my business doing the printing work for books and magazines. I came to realize the better blunt was in publishing, so I've hired a few sharp pens and began publishing my *Ladies' Journal* some years back. It's a comer, Miss Nesbitt, aimed at ladies like yourself, who want more from life than to be chained to a stove, rearing children. I thought from your article you were a modern, enlightened lady."

My hackles rose gently and I said, "I am."

He hopped up on the edge of his desk and with feet dangling from incredibly short legs, he smiled down at me. "I saw in you the logical successor to Mary Wollstonecraft—the lady who wrote *The Vindica-*

tion of the Rights of Women in the last century. There is a beacon waiting to be taken up, Missie, and a fortune for the lady who has the wits to grab it. There is a growing legion of women like yourself, fed up with being treated as ladies."

This was hardly the way I would have described my views, but I listened avidly. Having burned my bridge behind me, I had little choice. When he shoved a magazine under my nose, I felt myself slipping back into my dream world. It was the October issue of *The Ladies' Journal,* ready for distribution. Emblazoned on the cover in large black print was the title of my essay, "A Daughter's Dilemma," by ?. He had changed Anonymous Lady to that coy question mark. Somehow it hinted at a great mystery. A question mark could be anyone. A royal princess run amok, Lady Caroline Lamb, Madame de Staël. The possibilities were endless, and intriguing.

That the article was so prominently displayed did not suggest it was written by an unknown provincial like myself. The cover was illustrated in a cheap and garish way that shocked me. A buxom young woman, who would never in a million years be mistaken for a lady, was bursting free from chains, as well as from the top of her gown. In smaller print there was a lure to draw in the reader. "What does a young, beautiful lady do when she is thrown penniless into the world?"

I heard a sharp gasp and Annie exclaimed, "Oh dear!" in shocked accents.

"This is not the way your magazine looked last month, Mr. Pepper," I said weakly.

"No, it is changing every issue, following the trend suggested by my readers. It began with the sort of stuff you just handed me—pretty descriptions and poems and fashions and recipes. Other publishers are doing that better than I can, so I have opted for a different tack. You will be familiar with Mrs. Speers. She is my top writer, to judge by the letters. She writes in your vein, but not nearly so well. She writes about the downtrodden plight of ladies today."

The name was familiar. Her marble-covered novels littered the shelves of the lending library at Milverton. "I thought she was a novelist." And not one of my own favorites either.

"She used to scribble gothics, but she has run dry in that line."

"Do you feel there are enough ladies interested that you can make a go of this?" I asked doubtfully.

"You'd be surprised how many there are, and where they are hiding. Everyone from mousy housewives in the provinces to bored peeresses have written praising me." He glanced carelessly at the litter of papers on his desk. A quick peep showed me there wasn't a letter amongst the lot. It was proofs for his magazine that were strewn about there.

I was quite simply struck dumb at what he was suggesting. My fit of anger had been dissipated by pouring out all the spleen in that one essay. To have to rehash the same thing, month after month, seemed impossible. Yet to walk away with no possibility of future earnings was even worse. London had rejected my first essay. I knew the two efforts Pepper was holding were uninspired. I hadn't even enjoyed writing them. What to do?

"Think about it," he said. "I know you have it in you to be a literary star, Miss Nesbitt. It is infamous the way you were left out of your da's will. Aren't you interested in righting such wrongs as you see about you?"

"Yes."

He tossed up his hands. "There you are, then. Let me see anything you write. The payment will rise as you pick up your audience. I don't waste money on overhead, as you can see. After we have a collection of a couple of dozen essays, I see it going into a proper book. Anything in the way of fiction on the subject will be welcome as well. I have a line of ladies' novels—cheap gothics for the most part, but once you are established, I will put you out more handsomely."

My mind was reeling with such future glory. A star in the literary firmament, collections of my essays. No wonder if I sat mute. It was Annie who got us out of the office.

"We'll let you know," she said, and rose huffily to her feet.

Pepper hopped off the desk and walked us to the door. "Are you staying in town a spell, ladies?" he asked.

"Yes, I am moving to Bath," I replied.

"Ah, excellent! I do like to have my writers about me. I have persuaded Mrs. Speers to move here as well. A widow lady. I am calling on her this evening. She would be thrilled to meet you, Miss Nesbitt. She admired your essay violently. 'I wish I had written that!' she said when I showed it to her. She is a widow lady, turfed out of her home like yourself when her husband cocked up his toes and died."

"I dislike to call uninvited."

"We are not so niffy-naffy in our manners. All my

writers are one happy family. You will meet a half dozen of them at Lily—Mrs. Speers's do this evening. She enjoys throwing literary soirées. Bring along your chaperone if you dislike to come alone," he suggested with a quick glance at Annie.

I felt a pleasant humming of the blood in my veins at the words "literary soirée." It was the very sort of thing I had hoped to become involved in. Lily Speers was not a writer whose novels received wide critical acclaim, but certainly she was popular and prolific.

"Do you have her address?" I asked.

"I have one of her cards here somewhere," he said, and began rooting through his pockets, which held a whole packet of cards. It occurred to me that I must have new cards and stationery printed up as soon as I had found myself a set of rooms.

Mrs. Speers's dog-eared card was eventually found and handed over. I put it in my purse and we left, with every expression of pleasure at the visit, and assurance of meeting that evening at Mrs. Speers's house.

When we gained the fresh air and sunshine, Annie rolled up her eyes and said, "We'll catch the coach back to Milverton tomorrow. You won't want to have anything more to do with the likes of Pepper."

Her imperative glance told me she expected a battle, and I was happy to oblige her. "Nonsense. What does it matter to us if he chooses to live in a pigsty? We'll never have to come here again. It leaves all the more money to distribute to his authors."

"Aye, and have their works put out into the world with naked women on the cover. Your papa would roll over in his grave if he saw it."

"He's not likely to see it, is he, Annie? Ah, excellent! The cab waited for us, and I didn't even ask it to."

"How could it leave, when the road is full of cows? We shall be here all night."

After I had won the argument about remaining in Bath and continuing to write for Mr. Pepper, our talk turned to finding rooms. Annie was so disgruntled that I decided to put it off till tomorrow. With the lure of riches and stardom reeling in my head, I felt it not an extravagance. And besides, I wanted to spend some time planning my outfit and hairdo for Mrs. Speers's literary soirée.

Chapter Three

As THE RISING star in Mr. Pepper's literary firmament, I felt I had to dress the part. Not for me the modest frumpiness of Miss Burney or Jane Austen. I had seen pictures of Madame de Staël and Caroline Lamb, and was undecided which style to follow. A long examination of my face in the mirror hinted that the somewhat gamin charm of Lady Lamb was not for me. A turban, on the other hand, à la Staël, might add an aura of distinction.

That I did not possess a turban caused a delay, but by no means a deterrent. My elegant rose silk shawl, shot through with gold threads, would provide makeshift headgear till I could purchase a real turban. Lacking a proper brooch to tether the ends, I borrowed Annie's paste circlet of diamonds given to her by her niece last birthday. I seemed to recall that in the picture of Madame much admired in *La Belle Assemblée,* she wore an extremely decoletté gown to very impressive effect. Lacking her thoracic development (and a very low-cut gown) I settled for my green sarsenet. My shawl-turban usually provided warmth with that particular gown. As I possessed no suitable substitute, I decided to leave my arms bare, and hoped that Mrs. Speers kept a warm house.

My entire toilette was accompanied by a threnody from Annie, who insisted God in his heaven had nothing better to do than devise some hideously cruel fate for my waywardness. She courted redemption by wearing black, even if she was going to a party. I hoped it might be mistaken for a lack of interest in fashion, but really she looked like a carrion crow.

E'er long, the crow and the peacock were heading below stairs to our waiting hansom cab. I gave the driver the address, Lampards Street, and he moaned. "I'll try if I can coax my nags up the hill," he said in a voice that suggested it was downright cruel of us all, and not likely of success either.

The nags set out briskly enough, but as we began to scale the heights, our speed slackened noticeably. We were going so slowly as we crawled up Russell Street that there seemed a very real possibility we might have to get out and push. Eventually we were deposited at the doorstep of a large and fairly impressive-looking mansion, done in the Palladian style. Lights beamed from a dozen windows on three floors, giving a cheery aspect.

"You see what can be wrought by the power of the pen, Annie," I said, examining the house. "With luck and diligence, you and I may inhabit such a mansion one of these days."

"Make sure you don't build it atop a mountain like this one" was her sulky reply.

"But only look how lovely the view is," I pointed out. Below us spread the city, with lights gleaming like fireflies in the blackness of a summer garden. "By day it must be stunning. I shall compliment Mrs. Speers on her location."

"I doubt that poor team will ever stagger back down the hill without breaking their knees. With all the good flat land around, whoever decided to build a town in such an unlikely place?"

"I believe the Romans are responsible," I replied tartly, and headed to the door before she lured me into her bad mood.

The first intimation that all was not of the first stare chez Mrs. Speer was the squid-faced female servant who answered her door. In such an establishment, I expected a proper butler. The awful thought flashed into my head that till I had prospered beyond five guineas, Annie would be opening our door to my callers.

The girl, who had no more notion how to answer a door than a yahoo, curtsied, grinned, and said, "La, more company! Come in and join the squeeze, ladies, but don't expect to find a chair."

On this peculiar greeting we entered. The girl pointed to a table in the hallway, which was piled high with coats, curled beavers, walking sticks, gloves, bonnets, and pelisses, and disappeared without announcing us. Annie and I exchanged a blank stare and removed our outer garments. We stood in the hallway, peering into a brightly lit and noisy saloon, where perhaps two dozen people stood, holding glasses and shouting at each other at the top of their lungs. None of them, including the hostess, paid the slightest attention to us.

Annie looked at me, picked up her bonnet, and said, "If we hasten, we can still catch the cab."

A line from Shakespeare's *Julius Caesar* darted unbidden into my head. " 'Ambition should be made of sterner stuff,' " I said, and took a deep breath preparatory to announcing myself. It seemed an absurd thing to do, but how else was I to call the hostess's attention to our arrival? Surely a self-announcement was better than none.

I stood a moment, scanning the crowd. I need not have worried I was going a bit far to turn my shawl into a turban. I would have felt undressed without it. Every single lady in the room wore a turban. Nine tenths of them were topped off with towering plumes. None of the ladies carried shawls, and Madame de Staël's decoletté would not have rated a second glance. There were jewels aplenty, but even at a distance of three or four yards from the closest gem, I detected a noticeable lack of luster. Paste! If that red stone the size of a greengage plum had been a real ruby, it would be famous throughout the land.

After this observation, I turned my attention to the black jackets. There, too, things were amiss. The white shirtfronts and cravats did not sparkle as freshly laundered linen should. The jackets of the elders did not so much cling to shoulders as sag wearily from them. The younger gentlemen with some interest in fashion had their shoulders wadded out to ridiculous widths. Their hair was curled artfully over their foreheads, and one wore an outmoded pair of breeches and silk stockings. It was a parody of a polite party that called up, for some reason, the progress of Hogarth's rake.

I couldn't decide whether to laugh and join them or grab my pelisse and run out the door. Before any decision was taken, Mr. Pepper shot out from behind a laughing group and headed for me. I was surprised to see he owned a decent evening suit, and had a fresh shave. A statuesque lady of magisterial bearing tagged along behind. She wore a shiny green satin turban with white feathers, a huge brooch of strass glass, several square inches of gooseflesh, and a green gown. I judged her to be a well-seasoned forty-five or six, under her orange rouge.

Without waiting for introductions, she seized my two hands and pulled me against her ample bosoms. An awful stench of lavender and gin engulfed me. "Miss Nisbitt. How I have bin looking forward to meeting you. Arthur has told me all about you," she said in some strange accent that resulted from trying to hide the bells of Saint Mary le Bow by pursing her lips daintily. I escaped her clutches, and saw she was smiling at Mr. Pepper, presumably Arthur.

I presented Miss Potter, who was welcomed with a glancing nod, before Mrs. Speers, the lady in the green turban, clapped her hands and called for attention. A few curious heads turned to examine me while I was presented as "the lady we have all bin on nittles to meet, Miss Nesbitt." I shall not continue with her accent, but if you picture her lips pursed up as if she had sucked a lemon, you will have an idea how she spoke.

The lackluster eyes took a quick, disinterested glance, and returned to their shouting. "We shall escape this mad throng and have a quiet little cose," Mrs. Speers decided.

On that speech, the hostess deserted her party and led me to a morning parlor, where she called for wine and biscuits. I looked helplessly over my shoulder at Annie, and saw that Mr. Pepper was endeavoring gallantly to entertain her. At least he was handing her a glass of wine. What they would have to say to each other I could not imagine.

There was a grate in the parlor to which we went, but no fire in it. I felt goose bumps rise on my arms, and hoped the wine would allay the cold. It did not, nor did it provide any other pleasure. It posed as sherry, but tasted like turpentine. After the first sip, Mrs. Speers wisely set hers aside and called for water. What came was a colorless liquid bearing the telling aroma of juniper.

"Call me when Paton arrives, Sal," she said to the servant, the same one who had admitted us to the house.

"What a lovely big house you have, Mrs. Speers," I said, rather wondering why we were sequestered in such a cubbyhole of a parlor.

"There is no investment like real estate," she assured me. "When Gaby died—that is my late husband—he said, 'Lily, scrape up every penny you can lay your hands on and buy yourself a house. You will always have a roof over your head, and will never starve to death when you have a house with rooms you can let.' And I followed his advice." She took a long draught of her "water" and smacked her lips.

"I expect that was some time ago?" I queried politely.

"Oh my yes, a dozen years. I have grown rich since then. I have rooming houses sprinkled all around the country. I keep a room in each for myself, which makes traveling so much cheaper. I wrote *Angelina* in Newquay—in Cornwall, you know. I needed the stormy sea and cliffs and whatnot for that one. And

Marie Claire was written in Brighton, for she was an orphan from the Revolution."

"These are your gothic novels, Mrs. Speers?"

"Indeed they are. I wrote two dozen of them, and very profitable they were too, but I have taken up *serious* writing now."

"Indeed! For Mr. Pepper, you mean?"

"Pepper?" She stared, offended. "Certainly not, though I scribble up the odd article for him. Seven guineas always comes in handy to buy knick-knacks." Her eyes slid to the juniper water. "No, I am writing a biography of my heroine, Madame de Staël, Miss Nisbitt." Her voice was beginning to slur.

I had rather wondered that Mrs. Speers did not resent my rising star at *The Ladies' Journal,* and I now had my answer. I also had an idea what price to demand for my next essay. It seemed shockingly high. Throughout the conversation, Mrs. Speers's eager desire to meet me did not lead her to ask any questions, or even give me much chance to volunteer any information. Her real interests were twofold: herself and Madame de Staël, in that order.

When she next stopped to take a tipple, I put the pause in her monologue to good use and enquired, "What sort of article do you think Mr. Pepper wants?"

"Just the sort of thing you wrote before. That will go down very well, my dear. All about how men abuse us and steal our money under the guise of marriage, and leave us to educate ourselves. They take all the good jobs. Why should not Madame de Staël with all her learning and nobility and experiences, be an ambassadress, I should like to know?"

"Why indeed? But about my writing—to go on

writing the same sort of thing time after time . . ."

"It is what he wants. Millie Pilgrim writes on the plight of governesses and house servants. Her article on how the lords of the manor prey on innocent young girls was very effective. Next month she is doing nursemaids. Elinor Clancy, a vicar's orphan, writes of the situation of ministers' female children. There is more goes on in a rectory than counting prayerbooks! She knows of a vicar in Northumberland who has never opened a Bible. He has a daughter write all his sermons while he takes the bows and collects the money. That is the sort of thing we expose."

I felt quite at a loss. "I have no experience of that sort, I'm afraid."

She grabbed my hand and laughed gaily, "Oh, my dear! That is not what *you* shall write! You are so refained—I noticed it at once when Arthur showed me your essay. All done in lovely copperplate writing, and with such faine grammar. You are to write of life from the real lady's point of view. You will add a touch of class to the magazine. Such things as forcing daughters to marry for money, and how husbands squander their wives' blunt on other ladies—that sort of carry-on must be exposed. Surely you know of many such cases outside of your own, and if not, you must use your imagination. No need to mention any names at any rate, and go making enemies in high places. It will be the makings of you—and your friends need never know, for you will remain a question mark. My suggestion, by the by. Do you like it?"

"I thought it very clever, Mrs Speers. A definite improvement over the well-worn 'Anonymous Lady.' "

I saw that I had fallen into shameful company. But beneath all the awful vulgarity and self-seeking of the conversation, there was a kernel of justice. Wrongs were being perpetrated against my sex, and there was nothing immoral in exposing them. Quite the contrary, it ought to be done. Millie Pilgrim had taken up the cudgel on behalf of servants, Elinor Clancy on behalf of vicars' daughters—why not Emma Nesbitt on behalf of wronged genteel ladies? And of course I had urgent need of the money.

"And where are you staying, dear?" she enquired.

"At the Pelican."

"Samuel Johnson." She nodded. "But an inn is only for the nonce. You will not want to pay out such a stiff sum for long. You need rooms."

"Yes, I have been looking."

"Look no further," she announced, and smiled benignly. "A flat on my upper story has just been vacated. Four bright, airy rooms, furnished as faine as a star, and supplied with all incidentals. Linen, dishes, pots and pans aplenty. All of it going for an old song. Two guineas a week, including fuel for your grates. You will find the company congenial—all of us here are writers. Elinor has the other half of the upper, and Millie Pilgrim is below. Both jolly gels, and Elinor is very genteel. Mr. Bellows, an ill-feathered young owl, has half the second floor. He was up at Oxford for one term, and is Arthur's proofreader. Just between the two of us, Millie is unsteady in grammar and spelling, but Bellows polishes her up dandy. He also contributes the odd poem in a satirical vein. His *Sara Agonistes* was quite a hit. From Milton, you know."

My first reaction was that I would sooner live in a

cellar than with this house of hacks. A brief reflection of the morning's search, however, brought second thoughts. Four rooms sounded quite luxurious, and four furnished rooms at two guineas a week was a godsend. It would take some jawboning to talk Annie around, but I said, "I should like to look over the rooms in daylight. Shall we say tomorrow at ten?"

"Tin it is. I cannot be interrupted during my working hours, but I'll have Sal show you the rooms. You'll not find better at the price, Miss Netter." The bottle of water was lowering noticeably in the pitcher.

"It sounds reasonable."

"Where is Paton? Is he not here yet?" She yanked the bell cord and Sal, the butler, came running.

"He's here! What a swell, Mum! An out and outer!" was her manner of announcing Mr. Paton.

Mrs. Speers struggled up from her chair. Her step was unsteady as she headed for the door, looking from the rear like a shiny green hippopotamus wearing feathers on its head. "He is come to interview me for the *Quarterly Review*," she announced grandly. "Such an honor. I didn't half believe he would come, for he sent no reply to my invitation. No doubt that lummox of a Sal lost it."

She lurched out the door, and I sat on alone, wondering if I was imagining things. The prestigious *Quarterly Review* was actually taking Mrs. Speers seriously? They usually reviewed Walter Scott, Lord Byron, Roger Moore, and such luminaries. This literary life was a strange affair. And now I was to become a part of it. Whatever else it proved to be, it certainly was not dull.

Chapter Four

M<small>RS</small>. S<small>PEERS</small> <small>WAS</small> escorting Mr. Paton to her parlor as I made my way to the saloon. We met in the hallway. She did not stop to make us acquainted, but I heard myself being described as "a very refained young lady writer" as I turned the corner. The glimpse I had of Paton put me in no hurry to leave the party before he joined it. Quite apart from the good a review in the *Quarterly* could do my career, the highly polished article at Mrs. Speers's side interested me. To my astonishment, Annie was ensconced on a sofa with Pepper when I returned to the saloon, sloshing down a glass of Mrs. Speers's poison elixir. She was actually smiling! What on earth could Pepper be saying to her? She hadn't smiled since we left home.

I hurried forward and was offered a seat. "Mr. Pepper was just telling me about Ireland, Emma," Annie explained. "He comes from Doneraile, not far from where I was born. Can you imagine such a coincidence!"

Well, that accounted for the smiles. Mr. Pepper hadn't an Irish name, and there was no hint of the brogue in his voice, but he had at least been born on the ould sod, and green blood was always enough for Annie.

"I've bought back the old homestead," he said, smiling lazily. "My parents are dead now, but I mean to retire there one of these days, after Miss Nesbitt has made me rich."

"Made us both rich, I hope," I replied.

"Let me get you a glass of wine, Miss Nesbitt," he offered.

"No, thank you!"

He laughed merrily at that. "Not Lily's poison. I keep my own case in the cellar." There was a bottle on the table in front of them, and he poured me a glass of quite decent sherry.

We chatted a moment more about Ireland, then I said, "Did you know Paton, from the *Quarterly Review*, is interviewing Mrs. Speers? He was just shown in."

"You mean *Lord* Paton," he corrected me.

I felt a happy ringing in my ears. A lord! This was flying very high indeed. Annie and I exchanged a look of delight.

"I knew she was expecting him," Pepper continued. "I hope she is not—feeling poorly," he said. This suggested her problem was a chronic one. Pepper looked flustered, Annie looked curious, and I looked knowing.

"Not too badly," I assured him.

"It's the gin," he explained with an apologetic glance at Annie. "She never has a drop till she has finished her day's writing, but from three or four on, she tipples rather heavily, I'm afraid. She says her greatest story inspiration comes after a few drinks.

She promised to hold off today because of her party. The poor creature has seen all of life. She used to be pretty. Now she looks ridiculous, mutton dressed as lamb." He smiled appreciatively at Annie's accoutrements of grief. "But she can still write up a storm."

"I trust *you* won't have to resort to the bottle, Emma," Annie joked. Her joking about such a matter showed me she was enjoying herself, and I was glad, since I still had to tell her we were moving to Lampards Street.

"I understand it is her life of Madame de Staël that Paton is interested in," I continued. My real aim was to turn the conversation back to Paton, with hopes of garnering a review myself.

"Oh, certainly. The *Quarterly* would never condescend to do a critique of *my* magazine or writers," Pepper said. "They hold themselves too high for that."

Disappointment lent an edge to my voice. "That sounds grossly unfair to me!"

Pepper replied with a certain heat, "I wish you would tell Paton so!"

We stayed talking for perhaps ten minutes, during which time Pepper did not suggest introducing any of the guests to us, nor did any of them approach our corner except Mr. Bellows, the proofreader. The others were content to stare in an ill-bred way. It seemed a strangely uncivilized way to carry on at a party, but I was not in the least eager to rub elbows with any of them. The miscellany of accents heard and the frightful appearance of the gathering was enough to make a lady blush to be caught in their company.

I kept a sharp eye on the hallway, and soon spotted Mrs. Speers showing a wooden-faced Paton to the front door. He did not intend to mix with the hoi polloi then. I thought he had probably made short shrift of Mrs. Speers once he got a smell of her breath. I felt a little stab of disappointment. He was the only respectable person there, and now he was leaving. Across the room, I got a good, long look at him as he said a few words to Mrs. Speers.

He was not startlingly handsome by any means, but there was a quiet elegance about the man. His hair under the hall lights was the color of dry hay in the sun, a pale gold tinged with a glint very like silver. It was an uncommon shade, not unattractive. He wore it short, smooth to his well-shaped head. I could see his eyes were very dark, but their exact color escaped me at that distance. His face overall looked intelligent and rather pale. The man was no Corinthian. His height was a little above average, but appeared greater due to his lean, graceful body. Yet there was nothing of the man-milliner in his frame. He had good wide shoulders.

As I gazed, he lifted his quizzing glass, held it to his eye, and made a leisurely examination of the room. I was curious to see his reaction, which prevented me from averting my glance before he looked at me. His disinterest was humiliating. He passed me over with no more regard than if I were a dirty glass on the table. I had expected him to recognize my superior breeding instantly. In the mind's fancy I had already imagined us sharing a laugh at the infamous party where we had met as he praised my essay. Surely I appeared in a different light from all these turbaned women?

Except, of course, that I too was wearing a turban, pinned in the style of the party with a paste brooch. He could not see when I was sitting down that my gown was of excellent cut and material. No, what he saw was another aging writer in a demmed turban, sliding now over one eye at a rakish angle. In a moment he would leave, and surely never again set foot in this establishment.

I looked to Pepper and said, "Why do you not go and ring a peal over Lord Paton for ignoring your magazine, sir? I doubt you will have another opportunity."

Paton's glance slid back to our party, but I fear Pepper was the attraction. He nodded at Pepper, said a word to Mrs. Speers, and before I had time to straighten my turban, she was leading him toward us. I felt a blush creep up my neck and surreptitiously reached up to my head. I felt the unmistakable threads of the fringe working their way loose, and probably hanging out to betray the turban's origins.

Mrs. Speers and her victim were upon us. The hostess, quite slurry in her speech now, said, "You know Mr. Pepper, I think, your lordship. And this is Miss Nicols, so refained. We are delighted to have nabbed her for our periodical. Ladies, Lord Paton." Why she found it necessary to bow herself I do not know, but bow she did, more deeply than his lordship. Her feathers brushed Annie's nose. Annie batted them away angrily.

So many thoughts swarmed over me at once that I hardly knew what to say. The fringe was definitely loose, and beginning to tickle the back of my neck. Lord Paton's eyes were brown, a deep, rich brown like Dutch chocolate. He must think Mrs. Speers had no upbringing, calling him "his lordship," like an upstairs maid. His breeding overcame any propensity he must have felt to laugh at this charade.

He said, "Delighted to meet you, Miss Nicols."

"This is my cousin, Miss Potter," I said, pointing to Annie, who smiled very politely and murmured something.

No one seemed to notice or care that I had become Miss Nicols. I quite welcomed the alias and said nothing about the mistake.

"Miss Nesbitt has just been wondering why you never review *The Ladies' Journal,* Lord Paton," Mr. Pepper said archly.

Lord Paton, in forgivable confusion, looked about for Miss Nesbitt. "We seldom review magazines, Mr. Pepper," he explained. His voice was well modulated, firm, and authoritative without infringing on arrogance.

I recalled very clearly reading something about the *Edinburgh Review* in a recent issue of the *Quarterly* and said, "They will be surprised to hear that at the *Edinburgh Review!*"

The chocolate eyes settled on me with an air of surprise. No doubt he thought I spent all my time reading Mrs. Speers's gothic novels. "I said *seldom,* Miss Nicols, not never. One can hardly ignore an attack on such an acknowledged genius as Coleridge."

"Especially when his nephew is on the board of the *Review,*" Pepper riposted.

Mrs. Speers eyed the wine bottle and said, "You fool no one with that line, your lordship. We are ignored because we are ladies."

A sparkle of amusement lit Paton's eyes. "Now, you must know, Madame, a gentleman never ignores a lady."

"Except in print, eh?" she said, and gave his arm a nudge with her elbow. "Let us sit down before we all fall down." Her hand rose, ready to make a rush at the wine bottle. "Milord, I would be deeply honored if you would take a glass of wine before leaving."

"Thank you, I really must be going," he said hastily. I assumed he had already been served his draught of turpentine.

Mrs. Speers looked in some danger of falling over. To forestall this embarrassment, I rose and gave her my seat beside Annie, and the three elders began chatting, quite ignoring Lord Paton.

I smiled wanly at such a wretched display of poor breeding and said, "Will you be doing an article on Mrs. Speers's life of Madame de Staël?"

"Perhaps, when it is published. I was under the misapprehension that I was to receive a pre-publication copy this evening. It turns out, however, that the work is far from completion. I understand you are also one of Pepper's writers, Miss Nicols?"

"Nesbitt."

"I beg your—ah, that explains the mystery."

Mrs. Speers, who I hoped had passed beyond speech, heard the question and answered for me. "Miss Nevins is very genteel. She is to write about the lot of ladies. You never saw such a dainty fist as she writes."

The turban, mine, I mean, though Mrs. Speers's was also sitting aslant, was getting quite out of control. One end had worked loose and was falling like a misplaced tail down the back of my head. This annoyance, added to Mrs. Speers's claim for my gentility, made me blush bright pink. With an astonished and amused Lord Paton pretending to notice nothing amiss, I pulled the fringed tail over my shoulder and held it, as though it were a shawl.

"I take it you are familiar with the *Quarterly Review*, Miss Nesbitt," he said. His dark eyes roved the room.

"Yes, Papa subscribed to it when I was at home."

The roving eyes returned to me. "And now that you have, apparently, left home, I hope you will subscribe yourself. I see an empty sofa by the grate. Shall we?"

Triumph and misapprehension and hope did swift battle in my bosom. Hope won out, and I smilingly accompanied him to the sofa. I hoped to accomplish two things before he left; firstly to convince him I was not of the same social stamp as the company in which he found me, and secondly to get a review of my article in the *Quarterly*. Much guile and flattery would be required to perform these two miracles, but I was ready to be as clever and insincere as necessary.

"You mentioned having left home, Miss Nesbitt. Is 'home' very far away?" he asked when we were seated.

"I come from Milverton, only a day away."

"It's rather unusual for a young lady to leave home and set up on her own. I expect you are staying with relatives in Bath?"

"I am with my cousin, Miss Potter." I glanced in her direction and saw Annie, that model of dour respectability, playfully fighting off Pepper's attempts to refill her glass. Mrs. Speers, in the throes of a nap, had her head lolling on Pepper's shoulder with her feathers splayed over his shirtfront and her mouth open. Altogether they presented a very model of aging dissolution. I expected Lord Paton to be shocked at this sort of carrying-on, but he smiled blandly.

"Have you been with Pepper's magazine long?" he asked.

"No, I shall be making my debut in the next issue."

He smiled again, more warmly. "I dare say you have some hard things to say about gentlemen. *The Ladies' Journal* is not usually kind to us."

I felt a compelling urge to pour out the whole story of the iniquity recently visited on me. He seemed an understanding man. If he had any milk of human kindness, he would assist my effort to earn a living. Yet to burden a total stranger with any intimate details was too vulgar. I said vaguely, "You may find my essay harsh. I was stinging from a—a personal injustice when I wrote it. Had I permitted time to soften my first anger, I might have dealt less strongly."

His voice was full of concern. "Men can be beasts, sometime. Was it a father, husband . . ." Sympathy glazed his dark eyes. I swear if we had been alone, he would have held my hand.

All in a fluster, I said swiftly, "Oh, I am not married!"

"I wondered, as Mrs. Speers seemed a little uncertain of your name. I thought perhaps you had recently divorced and reverted to your maiden name."

"Divorced!" I gasped. "Indeed no. My name is and always has been Miss Nesbitt."

"Your father, then, is the culprit? Disinherited, I take it?"

"Yes, I have suddenly found myself impoverished. It was ill done of him, though one ought not to speak ill of the dead."

Lord Paton looked surprised. "I did not realize your wounds were so recent," he said.

In a twinkling I realized the error. He thought that because I had no mourning weeds about me, my father had been dead for some time. I was strangely reluctant to let him know this was not the case. Flouting convention was all well and good when I did not care for the opinion of anyone about me. To behave with so little propriety in front of a thoroughly respectable gentleman like Lord Paton was less comfortable. I rapidly conned my options and settled on Cousin Geoffrey as an excuse.

"It was not just my father's will when he passed away a year ago that vexed me. There was a cousin involved as well. A male cousin . . ." I left it at that, and hoped with all my heart that Lord Paton would do likewise.

"He attempted to force an unwanted match on you?" he said. It was more an assertion than a question.

I nodded. "If my essay seems very strong, there was good reason for it, you see. I know you do not ordinarily review magazines, but—"

All his compassion dissipated, and he said firmly, "There are many kinds of writing, Miss Nesbitt. Some authors deal with universal human problems, like Shakespeare. The vacillation of a Hamlet, the ambition of a Macbeth, the aging of Lear. Such writing enlightens us regarding the human condition; it is called literature, and is for all time. Other writings are of interest to only a select group—I mean such books as gothic novels, put out by the Minerva and Pepper presses for the entertainment of ladies. They do not attempt to enlighten, but are meant to amuse. The *Quarterly* is interested in only the former. You understand. It is no slur on your talent."

This patronizing speech sent a hot lava gush of anger surging through me. "You would put Rousseau in the former group as well, I assume?"

"Certainly. Voltaire and Rousseau are the pre-eminent—"

"And pray what enlightenment are *ladies* to take from the Frenchman's so-called literature? He informed us that we are to be treated like moonlings. I defy that assertion. I did not write my essay to entertain or amuse anyone. I wrote it to enlighten women and men—I had no select group in mind. It deals with an eternal human problem that bedevils fifty percent of the human population. If those are the criteria that constitute literature, then it is a fit work for you to consider."

"There is really a little more to it than that," he said vaguely, with a weary eye, as though it were all too abstruse to be apprehended by a mere female mind. He batted a graceful white hand. "I am referring to style."

"You can hardly expect an essay to be written in blank verse. I was indignant. The style is blunt, but the content is very serious."

Lord Paton looked quite taken aback. "Then it must be startlingly different from anything else Pepper has published."

"You wouldn't know, as you have decided without ever laying an eye on it that it is akin to a gothic novel."

A flash of anger lit his eyes, though he was trying to control it. "Time is finite. The propensity for wo—people to run off at the pen seems infinite. There aren't enough hours in the day to read everything that is published. One judges by the tone of a publication. Well, for that matter, your essay is not even on the stands yet. How could I have read it? Send me a copy, and I'll have a look at it. If it merits attention, I'll do a critique."

"Buy it yourself! I'm a professional writer! Those who *can* write. Those who *cannot* criticize."

His eyes opened up at that. It was obviously the first time Lord Paton had been put in his place. On that uncompromising speech I rose from my chair and strode out of the room, my turban tail adding the final touch of degradation to a humiliating evening. I went to Mrs. Speers's morning parlor to compose myself. It was my intention to remain there until someone came and told me Lord Paton had left.

This took approximately two minutes. It was Pepper and Annie who came to me. "What on earth did you say to Paton?" Pepper demanded. The tone of demand was full of mirth. "He tells me I have got a tiger by the tail, and wants to see an advance copy of your essay."

"I had very little opportunity to say anything. He was too busy giving me a basic lecture on Shakespeare."

Pepper shook his head, still smiling. "Any slight on his scholarship would be an offense. He thinks he knows all there is to know about literature. He took a first in the classics at Oxford. I expect we'll be hearing from that young man again."

"I hope his manners have improved!"

"I hope yours have as well," Annie declared. "The only respectable parti at the soirée, and you have to offend him."

"Oh, it would not be romance Paton has in his mind," Pepper cautioned us. "He comes from a very old, very rich, very noble family. His da is a duke, and Paton is the eldest son, a marquess with half a dozen estates scattered here and there across the land. I doubt he'll marry lower than a duke's daughter. But that don't mean we can't put him to good use if he takes an interest in Missie."

"Let us go home, Annie," I said.

Pepper had a ramshackle old carriage, and drove us to the hotel. I felt terribly depressed. Paton's remarks told me the world's opinion of Pepper's magazine. It was considered light, and I suspect slightly scandalous entertainment, for bored ladies and such non-ladies as had learned to read. I suspected it was an anodyne for governesses and unhappy wives, like a gothic novel. If I were to write that sort of thing, and truth to tell I did not feel I had any guidance on the human condition to give the world, I would prefer to write gothics. Mrs. Speers said they paid well. I always had a good imagination. That would come more easily to me than endlessly repeating how genteel ladies were repressed by men and society.

Our money was fast dwindling away while we stayed at the Pelican. Rooms were very dear, and the only cheap ones discovered were under the roof of the sodden Mrs. Speers. We must remove there at once, first thing tomorrow. After which I must write up another essay or two to recoup some money. But I would also begin a gothic novel to end all gothic novels.

I felt I had my villain in any case. He would not be one of Mrs. Radcliffe's dark, menacing older men, but a smooth-looking lord whom the heroine (and reader) first mistook for a friend. He would not reveal his true nature quite so quickly as Lord Paton had done that night, nor would my heroine behave like such a ninnyhammer. She would not entangle herself in a web of duplicity, saying in so many words that her father had been dead for a year. Why had I said it? To give Paton a better opinion of me, or at least not a worse one than he already had.

If I had behaved better, he might have become a friend. He must have remarked that I was different from the others at the party, for he had suggested I join him for some conversation. He had seemed very sympathetic at first. I had tried to urge my essay on him too quickly. That was when the mischief began. But at least he had asked Pepper for a copy.

While I sat with my diary open before me, I indulged in a foolish daydream of glory. Lord Paton would admire my article. He would praise it to the skies, and I would become the next Frances Burney. I would be invited to Carleton House to meet the Prince Regent. I must buy a real turban.

I wrote briefly: Party chez Mrs. Speers, a popular novelist. Met Ld. Paton, a toplofty marquess who deigned to lecture me on literature. Amused at his pretentions. Doubt I shall meet him again.

Chapter Five

THE FIRST ORDER of business the next morning was to reveal to Annie Potter that I planned for us to reside at Lampards Street. I expected her to hack down the suggestion, root and branch. She took it much better than I expected. "Mr. Pepper suggested something of the sort," she said. "It is not what we are used to, but it will do for a stopgap till you make us rich. A pity it is so high up the hill."

I noticed that Annie set aside her black mourning bonnet and wore her regular autumn one with the pretty feathers.

The second order of business was to find a hansom cab and pair of nags strong enough to haul us up to Lampards Street. Mrs. Speers had already told me she was not to be disturbed at her work, but she had given Sal instructions to show us the rooms. They were about what I expected the attics of a mansion to be like. Far from elegant to be sure, but bright and spacious. The furnishings were such a miscellany as you will find in any place furnished from second-hand shops and auction sales. It hardly seemed possible the bone-freezing chill of the space could be heated up by the miserable grate in the saloon, but small grates had also been installed in both bedchambers.

I paid the two guineas on the spot, and we returned to the Pelican to bring our trunks to our new abode. The remainder of the morning was spent in unpacking and arranging our scanty belongings about the place. We went out for luncheon, and in the afternoon we went to Milsom Street to buy food and a few necessities such as candles and soap and a turban. Annie thought it nonsense for me to wear a turban when Lord Paton was not a day over thirty, and would take me for an ancient. At least he would not take me for an ancient with a tail growing out of her head, and besides, we would not be seeing him again.

After much argument with the stove and a few difficulties with burning chops, Annie served us a simple dinner. She did not cook at Nesbitt Hall, but she had done so in Ireland in her youth, and was a fair hand in the kitchen. We were both very much aware of the heavy, plain crockery and tin cutlery that came with the rooms. We had not even thought to buy wine to enliven our evening, but we felt we had accomplished a good deal for one day, and that lent an air of gaiety to our simple repast.

When it was done, I overrode Annie's strenuous objections and put on a tea towel to serve as an apron while washing the dishes. Over the next few days I learned an exceedingly disagreeable fact of life. Every bite taken had to be first purchased, then prepared, and worst of all, the dishes on which it was served had to be washed and dried and put away. When the frequent shopping trips and general housecleaning were added to these duties, it left me with much less time than I had anticipated for actually writing. And this with Annie doing three quarters of the work! She would gladly have done it all, but she was not a kitchen maid, after all. Making some money to hire a maid became a matter of increasing exigency.

In any free moments, I was at work on a heartfelt essay dealing with the awful tedium of women's work. Men were busily inventing steam engines and various machines to save themselves the labor of grinding wheat, sawing logs, and rowing or sailing boats, but where were the work-saving tools for the housewife? The washing dolly-tub with its wooden paddles turned by hand was almost more laborious than the washboard. Could not some minor genius invent a machine to peel potatoes and wash the dishes? Science, like art, had become the handmaiden of the male sex. Scientists were too busy inventing new engines of war to bother about the kitchen.

Pepper liked the essay immensely (but not enough to raise the payment), and even added an idea for the next issue's essay. He pointed out that men had devised plenty of frills to make my sex more pleasing to men. Rouge, perfume, all manner of jeweled bibelot and fancy textiles, but where were the inventions to lighten the labor of the unfortunate? No, their concern was to make us look like pretty dolls. I do not mean to infer that I abhorred pretty ornaments. Far from it, I loved them, but they should have come after the necessities.

With articles for the next two issues of *The Ladies'*

Journal written and sold, I had a little time free to begin my novel. The memory of my villain had faded by slow degrees till it was hardly a memory. No critique of "A Daughter's Dilemma" appeared in the *Quarterly Review*. It *did* feature a glowing review of the infamous Lord Byron's latest epic, *The Lament of Tasso*. I wouldn't pay a penny to buy it, and it was out at the circulating library. From the review, however, I gather it to have enlightened mankind as to the human condition, familiar and of lively interest to us all, of languishing in prison, full of grief for the lost love of a trollop named Leonora d'Este. I rather liked the name Leonora, and planned to steal it for the heroine of my gothic, so I got something out of it after all.

Lord Paton's visit and several other incidents were discussed with Mrs. Speers. She was available for rational discourse only between the hours of four and six. She worked till four, and imbibed juniper water for the remainder of the day, but till she had downed three or four glasses, she proved an entertaining landlady. A part of the entertainment was to see how she dressed. She always looked ready for a fancy ball, though she seldom went out. Silks, satins, lace—the woman spent a fortune on her back. She often took tea, at either our place or her own, and she was a mine of gossip, which she called "tips" for a beginning writer.

"You need expect no leg up from Lord Paton," she informed me stiffly. "It is Byron's latest rhyme he is puffing off this month, and never mind what atrocities made it necessary for him to run away from England. Those lords stick together like warm wax.

You would not want to have anything to do with Paton if he comes sniffing around, my dear. He is a famous flirt, and one in your position . . ."

My position appeared to intrigue Mrs. Speers unduly. Annie had let slip that my father was only recently dead. She was busy trying to figure out all the dramatis personae of my first essay, I think, but I gave her no help. She recognized that I was from a class above her own, and approved of me.

"Arthur tells me Paton's ladybird drives around in a rig pulled by cream ponies, and wearing a fortune in jewels," she continued when I did not respond to her hint. "Angelina, she calls herself. But she is through with Paton. I hear she has taken on a new protector who is even richer. Lucky wench!"

Annie bridled up and said, "It is odd Arthur did not mention it to me."

Arthur Pepper, that unlikeliest of all flirts, had become an object of animosity between my chaperone and Mrs. Speers. As sure as he came calling on us, Mrs. Speers would make an excuse upstairs, even if she had to interrupt her writing to do it. He soon overcame that nuisance by calling after seven, when she was too firmly in Juniper's clutches to mount the stairs.

"Why should he?" Mrs. Speers demanded haughtily.

"Because Lord Paton seemed interested in Miss Nesbitt," Annie said hotly.

Mrs. Speers smirked indulgently in my direction. "Miss Nisbitt is a very refained young lady to be sure, but Lord Paton will be seeking a wife from the nubility. Someone like Madame de Staël, if she were a little younger and not a foreigner. Her being a foreigner makes her an interesting heroine for my biography, however."

I wondered what Madame would say if she knew in what passionate prose she was being clothed. Heroine indeed, as if the work were another gothic novel. To my knowledge the only research undertaken was to read the old gossip columns of Madame de Staël's visit to London, and to study the map of Europe to follow her other peregrinations.

"Anne Louise was born in Switzerland of a very wealthy family," Mrs. Speers continued. She was ingenious in getting hold of the conversation and pulling it in Madame (Anne Louise to her intîmes) de Staël's direction. "I do hear her papa lent two million francs to the French government some years ago, which no doubt accounts for her being a favorite of Napoleon's."

One of the few items of common knowledge regarding Madame was that Napoleon particularly despised her. I had to wonder if Mrs. Speers had bestowed these gems of misinformation on Lord Paton.

"Are you writing anything else for Arthur at the moment?" Annie inquired.

"Now that he has found someone to replace me, I am able to concentrate all my efforts on Anne Louise's story. Age is getting the better of me, and I limit myself to one work at a time. Such a relief that Arthur has managed to find a genteel young lady to fill the gap. Some of his writers are just a trifle common, I fear. Young Millie, *par example,* did not return home last night." She nodded her head wisely. "I'd swear on a Bible she had a gent clambering up a ladder into her room the night before, though they were quiet about it once they hopped into bed. I won't have *that* sort of carry-on in my house. Damned if I will. Don't you agree, Miss Nisbitt?"

"I'm sure you are mistaken in her character, Mrs. Speers," I said. "Millie mentioned she was going to visit her sister yesterday. No doubt she remained overnight."

"And no doubt her sister—if she has one—was rattling up the ladder at midnight the night before."

"I didn't hear anything."

She simpered knowingly. "It is so refreshing to have a *real* lady to talk to. You never suspect ill of anyone, Miss Nisbitt, even when it is staring you in the face. I'm sure it is no odds to me who the trollop amuses herself with, so long as she pays up regular and doesn't land a squawling brat in on us. And now I must return to my work. Thank you for the tea, it was lovely, as usual. A new tea set, I believe?"

The heavy crockery had been replaced, along with the addition of a few other refinements, to the detriment of our savings.

"Yes, do you like it?"

"Very genteel, I'm sure. If you're not using the old one, I'll just get it out of your way. I have picked up a rooming house in London, and am busy furnishing it."

Annie and I exchanged an astonished glance. "The gothics," she explained. "They are still selling as fast as kippers on the street corner. One reads of their demise from time to time, but great literature always endures, don't you agree, Miss Nisbitt?"

I smiled pleasantly, and made a mental note to step up the pace on my own gothic. In order to catch the right, profitable tone, I borrowed a few of Mrs. Speers's novels. Outwriting her did not appear to pose a problem. I could invent a gloomy mansion borded by ancient yews, and a heroine prone to swooning at the slightest provocation as well as the next one. It was the heroine herself that upset me. Could any female really be so foolish as to believe in ghosts? Was sitting around, swooning, the only course of action to occur to her? Such a woman deserved her fate. Yet this was what allowed Mrs. Speers to buy up a rooming house with as little care for the expense as buying a new pair of stockings.

In the above manner we settled into our new life. At times we, probably Annie more than I, felt the loss of what we had left behind. On rainy days, of which there were many as September drew to a close, we felt like badgers in their sett in our shabby little rooms. But Annie had Arthur, I had my career, and we both had the satisfaction of independence.

We also had a flurry of letters from Geoffrey Nesbitt. The first contained an apology, in case he had unintentionally done anything to cause offense, and enquired in polite but stiff words how long we planned to remain in Bath. Our friends were pestering him for information, and he felt uncomfortable having to put them off for so long. Annie had written to him, giving our address. I wrote a reply, stiffer still than his own, ignoring any reference to having taken offense at the theft of my fortune, and informing him that it was not my intention to return, ever.

Three days later I received another missile, informing me that I was behaving irrationally, and asking what I was using for money. I replied that

Bedlam had not come after me yet, and I was using pounds, shillings, and pence for money. He took the gloves off in the next one and ordered me home immediately. I mentally composed half a dozen replies of cutting irony, but did not commit any of them to paper. I had decided to ignore Geoffrey Nesbitt. If any more unsolicited letters arrived, I would refuse to pay for them. Let the post office return them for all I cared.

My wrath was poured out in my diary. Here is a sample of it. You can skip over it if purple prose is not in your line. "At what point in history was it decided that females were the inferior sex? In A.D. 60 Queen Boadicea led an army against the Roman legions. Queen Elizabeth, centuries later, was still able to overcome the bias toward her sex. In two hundred years, we have sunk to mere ciphers. If I should try to gather up an army of women today, I wager I could not raise a single regiment in all the island, with Ireland thrown in. Victory must be achieved more cunningly. The pen is still mightier than the sword. We must take control of the pen."

Yet what my pen really wanted to write was a gothic novel. My heroine, however, would be instrumental in her own salvation. That would be one little step for womankind.

Chapter Six

WE HAD BEEN two weeks at Lampards Street. Between the exigencies of settling into our new rooms, my writing, the flurry of correspondence from Cousin Geoffrey, and finding our way about town, we had not done much in the way of establishing ourselves socially. We passed as quite the tip of the ton at Lampards Street, where the landlady and all the other denizens treated us with a comical degree of deference. We had made a few nodding acquaintances at the Pump Room, but there were larger fields to conquer, even in Bath. By degrees, Mr. Pepper and I had coerced Annie out of any semblance of mourning. Now it was time to enter our names with the Master of Ceremonies at the Assembly Rooms, and take on a wider society. Our first venture out was to a ball at the Upper Rooms.

During the day there was a flurry of refreshing our complexions with Gowland lotion and lemon water. Our hair was tied up in rags till the curls bounced in joy. Nails were filed and buffed. Gowns were pressed and all the other attempts at elegance attended to. The turban was to be abandoned for this public appearance. Miss Nesbitt would make her bows in an elegant golden gown of corded silk, the skirt rutched up with tiny dark green satin bows.

As Bath had the reputation of a valedtudinarians' haven, I anticipated a sedate party. Imagine my delight to see the throng of black jackets blocking the door. The heads above them were neither grizzled nor bald, but a pleasing variety of browns, blacks, and blonds. My anticipation for the evening soared as we edged our way into the room. I felt like a heifer on the sale platform, being ogled so blatantly by the mob.

"We shall just find a seat a little farther into the room," I said over my shoulder to Annie.

We inched forward, with "Pardon me" and "Sorry" sprinkled to left and right as we progressed. There was scarcely a seat to be had, but just before we came to the highest bench, a couple vacated their chairs, and with more speed than grace we beat another pair of ladies to them. I felt rather foolish when I realized one of the ladies was elderly, and rose to offer her my seat.

She was a toplofty-looking dame with a face like a gothic painting, but she smiled with great condescension and accepted the chair. Names were soon exchanged. The lady was a true Lady, one Lady De-Grue, and the young companion was her niece, Miss Bonham. While Annie conversed with the elder, I struck up a conversation with the younger. The ladies turned out to be regular inhabitants of Bath, and were imbued with its restraint. Miss Bonham, who was not more than a year or two younger than myself, wore her hair parted in the center and skinned back in a tight little ball. She was quite pretty, with regular features, but very shy. Her gown rose nearly to her collarbone, and its adornments were few.

I soon sensed that Miss Bonham was not the sort of person who would appreciate *The Ladies' Journal.* She was tediously proper, and I did not mention my career. Instead, I spoke of Nesbitt Hall. Naturally my father's recent demise was concealed. My permanent remove to Bath became a visit, and per force Annie became invalidish.

I trusted Annie was purveying the same story to Lady DeGrue. Before long, Miss Bonham found a partner in an elderly gentleman whom she addressed as Sir Laurence. Lady DeGrue accepted the escort of Sir Laurence's companion to the card parlor, and I finally got to sit down.

Annie immediately leaned toward me and said, "I hope you did not tell her anything about your writing. Lady DeGrue is a mighty high stickler."

It was soon sorted out between us that we had both told the same lies. This settled, I was free to cast my eyes hopefully over the gentlemen. Outside of possibly seeing Lord Paton, I had not thought I would know anyone there. I could not decide whether I was happy or otherwise, when Mr. Bellows came bolting across the floor. In case your memory needs refreshing, he is Pepper's owlish assistant, the man in charge of polishing up the prose of us writers before it appears in print.

He was undeniably a gentleman insofar as speech and manners go, and when that is said, the list of compliments runs dry. His father was a vicar in some village in the north of England. He attended

Oxford for a year, after which the money ran out and he had to take work. He was a bookish young man of twenty-two or -three years. Whatever Pepper paid him, it was not enough to keep up a creditable appearance. He looked and dressed like the impoverished son of a minor clergyman. He was of medium height and less than medium girth, not far from emaciated actually. His bony face, with dark eyes sunk deep into the sockets, always reminded me of a death's skull when I met him on the stairs at Lampards Street.

The awful idea was taking root that he mistook me for a lady of fortune, and meant to marry me. I don't know what else could account for his fawning manner.

"Miss Nesbitt! I have been hoping for weeks to find you here one evening," he said in a solemn voice. "May I have the pleasure of the next dance?"

A host of troubles rose up to attack me. I disliked to refuse outright, yet was loathe to have him set the tone for my possible partners. No doubt he was accompanied by other needy friends. I would be passed from one to the other, and kept from making more interesting acquaintances. On the other hand, I had not stood up since arriving. One was practically invisible when seated. Perhaps if I got on to the floor . . .

And then there was Annie. I could not like to leave her all alone. Just as I was turning to display my excuse for refusing, I spotted Mr. Pepper ducking forward, dodging through the crowd at top speed to claim Annie. I also noticed the upturning of her lips, the gleam in her eye.

I said, "I would be delighted, Mr. Bellows. Thank you."

Pepper said a few words and then suggested taking Annie away to the card room. I cast a commanding eye on her to remain where she was, but was forestalled by Bellows.

"Don't worry about your charge, Miss Potter," he said. "I shall consider it an honor to look after Miss Nesbitt."

There was the germ of an idea for an essay here. Why should I, at seven and twenty, require looking after, especially by an unlicked cub like Bellows?

"We shall meet for tea," Pepper said, and I was left stranded with Bellows.

I took what consolation I could from escaping the card party, and went with my partner to take my place in the set. There was not going to be one moment's pleasure in this entire evening. I knew it as surely as I knew the two rawboned, awkward-looking youths toward whom we were rushing were Bellows's friends. My next dances would be with them. I would ask Annie to leave as soon as tea was over.

Bellows was soon proudly presenting me like a trophy to the awkward youths and their partners. It was clear from their assessing eyes that I had been much spoken of. "So this is Miss Nesbitt!" and "Delighted to meet you at last" would have told the tale if their conspiratorial grins had not.

It did not seem to occur to any of them that our set lacked a couple, and the musicians' violins were already making those squawking sounds which presage the beginning of the music. I said not a word.

If we failed to fill the set, I might escape yet. The card parlor now seemed preferable to the dance.

"We need another couple here. Where is the M.C.?" Mr. Bellows said in a fine, taking-charge manner.

I smiled wanly and said, "Such a pity! It seems we cannot complete the set. Shall we retire . . ."

"Here's a chap and his lady now," Bellows said. "Why, it's Lord Paton!"

My heart sank to my slippers. I turned slowly and saw the unmistakable silvery-gold head and straight shoulders of Lord Paton gliding toward us. Any hope that he would not remember me vanished on the spot. His dark eyes were on me, and his lips were pursed in amusement. Within seconds he was presenting his partner, Mrs. Brisbane, to us. She was pretty, in a dashing way that fell just short of vulgarity. Her eyes were a shade too bright, her gown sprinkled with spangles, her voice just a touch loud, and her arm clung so tenaciously to Paton that it pulled his sleeve askew. I noticed she had the strongest possible effect on the provincial gentlemen in our set. That did not surprise me, but I had expected more discernment from Lord Paton.

The music began, and the dance proceeded before anything that could rightly be called conversation took place. The provincials made no headway whatsoever with the dasher. Her flashing eyes were only for Lord Paton. No matter what partner the movements of the dance gave her, her attention never wavered from him. He was too polite to ignore her, but he did not return his undivided attention. As often as not, he was looking at me in a strangely conspiratorial way that was hard to account for.

When the dance was over, he took Mrs. Brisbane

on one arm, myself on the other, and swept us off. "I have someone who is very eager to meet you, Miss Nesbitt," he said.

Mrs. Brisbane was returned to a chaperone and very civilly thanked for the dance. She managed to both smile at Paton and glare at me before we resumed our walk, which took us toward the doorway.

"Who is it that wishes to meet me?" I asked.

We were at the doorway. He opened it and ushered me out without answering my question. "Tea will be announced immediately. In this way, we beat the crowd and get our choice of table. That one in the corner—not the one by the doorway. We'd be jostled to death."

I noticed that the table to which he dashed was a table for two. Most of them accommodated larger parties. "I am supposed to meet my chaperone," I said.

"She is at cards?"

"Yes."

"Then she will wish to take tea with her group. You don't *really* want to listen to card talk for half an hour, do you? Useless repinings about trumps and tricks and honors?"

"But I said I would meet her."

He smiled urbanely. "I'll go to her table and explain."

He drew my chair. I sat down, and Lord Paton summoned a waiter by some magic, invisible means. He ordered tea and cakes, and I once again asked who wished to meet me.

"Me," he replied with a smile that would not only lure birds from a tree, but vultures from a carcass.

It was a peculiarly intimate smile that had more

to do with the eyes than the lips. It took me a moment to recover my wits, but eventually I said, "You mean it is all a trick? There is no one at all?"

"Only that sorry old critic, Paton. Practically no one."

The word "critic" jumped out of the conversation and into my mind. Was it possible he was going to review my essay after all? The next term's *Review* was probably being written now.

"And what does the critic think of my essay?" I inquired hopefully.

"It was a very spirited attack on masculine arrogance. It certainly made *me* think."

"Then you will give it a good review?"

His mouth, which had been formed in a smile till that moment, fell open in surprise. "Ah—well, I am only a scribe for the *Review,* you know. I do an occasional piece for them, but it is the editors who determine the contents, the works to be reviewed. I broached the matter of your essay. They felt it would not be of interest to our readers."

A weak "oh" was all I could manage. My hopes were dashed to the ground. "Why did you wish to meet me, then?"

Another of those intimate smiles glowed in his eyes. "I am not only interested in the anonymous writer, but in Miss Nesbitt herself."

The cakes and tea arrived, along with a sudden rush of customers into the room. We surveyed the throng till we spotted Annie and Mr. Pepper. They were with the rest of their card table, as Lord Paton had prophesied. He went and made my excuses to Annie, and returned just as I was setting down the teapot.

"I wish you had waited," he said. "I like to watch a lady pour tea."

"Drink up, then, and you shall see me pour the next cup. It is hardly a performance to anticipate. I lift the pot by the handle and tip, hopefully in the direction of the cup."

"But the curve of the wrist, the height at which the pot is held, are revealing. Is the pourer a venturesome lady who has confidence in her ability to hold the pot high and let the steaming liquid gush like a waterfall? Or does she let it hug the cup and trickle in with no flare? That is what I should like to have seen, Miss Nesbitt."

"This is a new method of character revelation, to read the pouring rather than the leaves. I shall be very careful at what height I hold this creamer. You go first, milord. I shall try to spoon the sugar into the cup unseen while you are occupied."

"I take my tea straight, but neither milk nor sugar count in any case. There is no threat in milk and sugar, except to the figure. Hot tea, on the other hand, is something to be handled."

I felt uncomfortable all the same as I poured the milk with his dark eyes observing me.

"I see you have put off your turban this evening," he mentioned after we had tested the tea and found it acceptable.

I felt a little blush at this reminder of the past. "Just as well. No doubt you noticed its eagerness to leave my head when last we met."

Paton put back his head and emitted a very natural-sounding laugh, deep and masculine. "You will never know what fortitude was required to prevent me from running after you and giving that tail a yank as you strode majestically from the party. You handled the contretemps admirably, by the by. I *do* admire a lady with a countenance."

"It wasn't a real turban."

"So I gathered. At least they don't usually come equipped with a fringe. I shouldn't think you care much—yet—for my opinion, but I think you look lovelier *sans* turban. Why were you so eager to don the disguise of an older lady?"

This brief, offhand speech gave me pause for thought. The "yet" suggested the time was coming when I would care for his good opinion. "Lovelier" gave rise to the hope that even *avec* turban I was not grotesque, and of course the suggestion that I was not an older lady was most pleasing of all.

"I did not wish to appear different from all the other literary ladies. Would you have me draw vulgar attention to myself by being the only one there without a turban and paste brooch?"

"A case of when in Rome . . ." He examined the pearls at my throat, which were genuine and not small. "I trust you will not feel obliged to succumb to all of Mrs. Speers's idiosyncracies."

"Neither gin nor Madame de Staël are amongst my weaknesses." This talk of weaknesses recalled to mind a certain Angelina, and a pair of cream ponies. I lifted a brow and said archly, "But perhaps we ought not to harp on weaknesses. We are none of us perfect, I think?"

His bland smile revealed nothing. If my shot hit home, it delivered no pain whatsoever upon impact. "Very true. I have never been at all good at geometry," he said. "My whist is only passable, and I am considered an indifferent hunter by my friends.

Those are my more outstanding defects. Will you reciprocate, Miss Nesbitt, and caution me of your imperfections? You will note my subtlety. I do not accuse a lady of actual weaknesses."

"Nothing to speak of. A touch of imperfection perhaps in six of the seven deadly sins. I acquit myself of gluttony."

He listened, smiling remotely. "But not the others—pride, covetousness, lust . . ."

"Good gracious! I was only joking!"

"I like a sense of humor in a lady. I think you and I are going to become very good friends, Miss Nesbitt."

This speech had something of the air of conferring a favor. It is hard to say just what accounted for it, unless it was the implicit assumption that my friendship was available for the taking. Perhaps it was Lord Paton's wealth and superior position in life that were to blame for his attitude, but my backbone stiffened, and my reply revealed nothing of the sense of humor recently conferred on me.

"Your friends require a sense of humor, do they?"

"Not at all. I am ridiculous enough to lure a smile from a Methodist, but you must own a glowering woman is no blessing to anyone."

"No, nor a glowering man either."

"I seldom glower, unless driven to extremity. It takes some such catastrophe as losing my fortune at cards, or a badly set cravat to put me out of sorts. Usually I am a model of smiling idiocy. But you must judge me after you have had time to see whether we suit. Shall we say tomorrow, around three-thirty, for a spin into the country?"

When I lifted the teapot to refill our cups, I had

other things on my mind than the pouring. Lord Paton appeared interested in me, and quite apart from the literary doors he might open, he was an excellent parti. His physical person was attractive, and he was amusing. There was no earthly reason to refuse.

"I have usually finished my writing by three. Three-thirty will be fine."

Then I noticed he was paying close attention to the pouring. "That was admirably done," he congratulated me. "Wherever you learned to pour tea, you do it with a ladylike air."

"I should hope so! I was not reared in the gutter, you know."

"You don't belong in an attic either, Miss Nesbitt. Pray, don't be angry that I have been poking my nose a little into your situation. I was interested in you from the moment we met."

It was hard to be angry at such a statement as that. In fact, I felt quite giddy with astonishment. "You have an odd way of showing it, sir. Two weeks have elapsed since first we met, and you have not called on me. If we had not chanced to meet here this evening, I doubt I would ever have seen you again."

"Now, there you are mistaken. I was not in a position to—to pursue the acquaintance at that time. I had some—er, personal affairs to tidy up. The two weeks have been used in paving the way for our friendship."

It seemed impossible that Lord Paton should blush and stammer like a schoolgirl, but blush and stammer he did. The personal affairs I immediately concluded were Angelina and her cream ponies. He had turned off his flirt. This sounded like serious business.

When he looked at me, I felt as though he was reading my mind. It was a deep, probing gaze, full of meaning. "You know what I am referring to, I think?" he asked.

"How should I? I am not a mind reader."

"Bath is a cauldron of gossip. A man cannot hope to keep anything secret," he said with a scowl.

"Then a man ought not to do anything he is ashamed of."

He lifted his quizzing glass and examined me with one eye magnified. "Not in Bath, in any case. Nor should a lady either, Miss Nesbitt." It seemed to be my gown he was staring at, though there was nothing amiss with it. It was not particularly revealing. "You look remarkably handsome in gold, though I think you could wear *black* to advantage as well. Not that a lady would appear at a ball in black, of course. That suggests she is in *mourning*." The enlarged eye held a challenge.

He knew. His nose poking must have led him to Milverton, or someone who knew me. I couldn't meet his gaze. I looked at the table, and noticed we had not touched the plate of cakes, which looked quite delicious.

Lord Paton's hand moved into my ken. It was a lovely hand, long-fingered, elegant, with a carved emerald on one finger. He raised his hand, and I felt it touch me under the chin, lifting my head till I was forced to look at him. He was saying something with his eyes, but it was not easy to read. There was compassion there, I think, but tinged with impatience, or anger.

"Tomorrow, at three-thirty," he said gently, and smiled.

The anger was for my father, then, and the stunt he had played on me. He had read my essay, and understood why I behaved with so little propriety. I felt close to Lord Paton at that moment. It was easy to forget he was a virtual stranger. When a handsome and very eligible gentleman singles out a lady of no particular significance, she does not feel him a stranger for long. She has known him for years, in her dreams.

We talked a little more about nothing in particular. Soon Mr. Pepper and Annie came to our table, and Lord Paton left. I urged Annie to go home before the ball was over, and as she has no love for late nights, she was happy to oblige me.

In the cab on the way up the hill she said, "Did you have a dance with Lord Paton, or just take tea with him?"

"He joined our set. He is coming to call tomorrow afternoon, Annie."

"You never mean it! Did he say anything about your writing?"

"The editors would not let him give me a review. He just writes for the magazine, he has nothing to say about choosing the subjects."

She gave me a coy look. "Then the friendship has nothing to do with your writing. That looks promising."

"Yes, it does," I agreed, and could hardly hold in a triumphant laugh. "It was a lovely ball, was it not?"

"Lovely. I won two shillings. I shall buy an evening purse. I saw a dandy beaded one on Milsom Street."

You may imagine what glorious thoughts danced in my head as I lay in bed that evening, waiting for sleep to come. I had been courted, betrothed, wedded, and taken my groom home to show off to Geoffrey within half an hour. Once this climax was accomplished, my thoughts turned to more soporific ones, viz., my novel. There was a deal of revising to be done there, turning the former villain into the hero. Most of it, I decided, could be done by a simple change of hair and eye color. My hero, Lord Havard, would switch his pate from jetty black to electrum, and his blue eyes to brown; my villain the reverse.

What would be more difficult was to keep my creative thoughts sunk in gloom. The leaden skies would be turning to blue if I was not careful. I hoped it did not rain tomorrow, to cancel my outing. God could not be so cruel, even if he was a man. Just before I slept, I remembered I had not written in my journal. I would rectify the omission tomorrow.

Chapter Seven

I AWOKE IN the morning with a sense of exhilaration whose cause was not immediately apparent. Then I opened the curtains and looked out at a beaming blue sky, and remembered my prayer for just this weather. I was driving out with Lord Paton! The morning was given over to working on my gothic, as that allowed me to put my daydreaming to use. There was much scratching out and substituting of black hair for blond, blue eyes for brown, which curiously, gleamed with interest, glowed and gazed lovingly as the story progressed. My villain, Mr. Jeffreys, remained a trifle unresolved, but the hero took solid shape and form. When I realized I had unwittingly given my villain the name of my scurrilous cousin, he, too, fell into sharp focus.

After lunch I began my toilette for the drive. My curls, with last night's bounce reduced to a jiggle, were pinned up behind in a basket. The contours of my face look best with only one frame, which my bonnet provided. With that sunny sky, there was no need for a pelisse over my worsted suit. To alleviate its severity, I wore a lacy fichu at the neck, with a cameo pin. The effect was somewhat akin to a governess, but not displeasing. With a memory of Lord Paton's Angelina and my own questionable behavior regarding mourning, I wished to flaunt my respectability.

The saloon in which I greeted Lord Paton certainly held nothing in the way of refinement, unless the presence of a chaperone can be called refined.

"You must forgive this place," I said as soon as Lord Paton entered. "It is not what you or Miss Potter and I are accustomed to, I fear."

His dark eyes darted hither and thither, trying not to exhibit the rampant curiosity he must surely have been feeling.

"The saloon at Nesbitt Hall is so grand and spacious," Annie mentioned. "Emma says she feels like a badger in its sett, cooped up here."

"It will take a little getting use to, I expect," he said blandly.

"Would you care for a glass of wine before we leave?" I inquired.

"Thank you."

Annie darted for the sherry. We had replaced Mrs. Speers's glasses with crystal stemmed goblets, and could serve the refreshment without blushing.

We had only one glass before leaving. "Isn't it a lovely day!" I exclaimed joyfully when we went out into the sunlight. It was made lovelier by the sudden appearance of Mr. Bellows and Millie Pilgrim, who were just alighting from a cab. They ogled us to death.

"Fine weather for badgers." Lord Paton smiled, and assisted me into a dashing yellow sporting curricle. "You will not feel cooped up in this rig, Miss Nesbitt."

It was certainly an elegant vehicle, in its own way. The team, too, were a prime pair of chestnut bloods. I was vain and foolish enough to wish it was his crested carriage, till it occurred to me that we would be more highly visible in the open rig. Heads would turn on Milsom Street when we darted along at the inevitable sixteen miles an hour that all drivers of prime bloods speak of.

Lord Paton assisted me on to the seat and took his own place. "You had best move in an inch from the edge," he suggested. "There is no danger on the straightaway, but the corners can be tricky."

"No doubt your nags are chomping to show off their speed. Sixteen miles an hour, I assume?"

"I don't like to boast, but they made it from Land's End to John O'Groats in ten minutes."

On this facetious speech he reached out, put his arm around my waist, and pulled me closer to him. That surprising action set the tone for the drive. It bordered on improper behavior, yet there was a reason—or at least an excuse for it. The walls of the seat were somewhat low.

"Ten minutes! Without bating the horses, and without losing any shoes, then, I assume?" I asked, trying to hide that I was flustered at being crushed up against his side. I shifted over till there were a few inches between us.

He watched me with a smile. "There was no need of shoes. They flew," he said, and flicked the whip over the nags' heads.

They were off, not quite flying, but with a lurch that gave my neck a sharp jar, and lifted my bonnet

72

an inch. Had it not been for the ribbons, it would have left my head entirely. I had thought we would descend the downs into the town proper. It was with a definite sense of disappointment that I realized this was not his intention.

"I thought we would be driving along the river," I said, hoping in this oblique way to alter his course. Was no one to view my glory except Millie and Bellows?

Lord Paton thought less than nothing of the river. "A cold wind blows off it in autumn, but if you care to see it, you can. The Avon curves north at the east side of town."

So it did, and I caught a quick glimpse of it as we hurtled down the road. Once free of the city, the nags settled down to a hundred or so miles an hour. As we proceeded in a northeasterly direction away from the coast, the river, the Mendip Hills, and all other scenic wonders that the vicinity offers, the sky joined in my mood and turned from blue to gray. Clouds were blown in on a brisk wind that cut through my serge suit like a knife through soft butter.

The glory of driving out with Lord Paton was seen by the driver of a cartful of turnips, a farmer with his wife and five children all squeezed into a donkey-driven gig, a mole catcher, and a pair of young boys playing truant from school. The occupants of the one respectable carriage we passed could not possibly have seen us for the cloud of dust they blew up into our faces. I removed my cramped fingers from the carriage edge long enough to draw out my handkerchief and bat at the dust.

"Perhaps we should turn back. It is getting quite cloudy," I pointed out.

"We're almost there."

"I don't believe you mentioned our destination."

"The whole area is pretty," he said vaguely. "Bowood Park is nearby, a handsome estate designed by the Adams brothers. It belongs to a friend of mine, Lord Lansdowne. Sloperton Cottage, where Thomas More spent his last days, is only a few miles away. Coleridge, the poet, is at Calne, also nearby—or was the last I heard. This is a fascinating area, with many interesting spots to visit. Badminton, too, is only a little north."

My mind reeled with all these intriguing possibilities. Was he going to call on his friend, Lord Lansdowne? What a story to take home to Lampards Street. Coleridge, a pre-eminent poet, was even better.

"Do you know Coleridge?" I asked hopefully.

"Oh, certainly. I have met him any number of times. A long-winded bore, and Wordsworth is worse. They are both better met in their poetry. Strange, is it not, how writers differ so markedly from their works? One would never have thought, to read 'A Daughter's Dilemma,' that you would be a charming young lady. Had I read your essay before meeting you, I would have expected a harpy."

This flattery, while welcome, added nothing to my physical comfort. We had been driving for the better part of an hour. The next milestone said Corsham, one mile. "We had best turn back," I suggested. I could no longer conceal the bouts of shivering that assailed me.

"We shall stop first and have tea. The wind is rising. Corsham is the closest village to—" He came to an abrupt stop, but soon continued. "Did I mention Lord Methuen lives at Corsham? A handsome old Elizabethan heap."

"No, you didn't." But he had mentioned Lord Lansdowne and Coleridge, and as no visit to these luminaries had transpired, I had no real hopes of taking tea with Lord Methuen—nor did we.

"Our destination is only a stone's throw from Corsham," he assured me.

I consoled myself that he *did* have a real destination in mind, and kept an eye peeled for either a noble heap of stones or a public inn. I observed a certain anticipatory gleam in Lord Paton's eye, and was taken with the idea that it was his own estate we were heading to. He was familiar with all the local landmarks, he was living in Bath, the closest city of any size.

"Where is your country seat, sir?" I inquired.

"Kent."

This killed the possibility that I was being rushed home to meet the family. It was one of his lesser abodes we were to visit then.

"How does it come that you live in Bath?"

"My father is still alive. He lives at Paton Hall. I spend most of my time in London."

"London! I thought you live in Bath."

He looked totally astonished. "Good God, no. Nobody lives in Bath. I am here only on family business. My mother's sister has some property in town she wishes to develop. I am staying with her a month to give her a hand. She is getting on, you know. I will be the eventual inheritor, and she asked my advice on the matter. We have decided to build a block of flats, as the demand is certainly there, and it will be more profitable than building three or four single dwellings."

"When—when will you be leaving?" I asked.

He turned his dark gaze on me. "I am in no hurry—now."

I thought, all the same, that he was in something of a hurry. There was an air of haste in this courting. We had proceeded another half mile, which is farther than any mere mortal can throw a stone. Surely our destination must be close, but the only building on the horizon was a little thatched cottage standing under the protection of a spreading mulberry tree. A welcoming puff of smoke came from its chimney. I was quite simply astonished when he pulled the reins and turned in at the lane to this modest dwelling.

"Do you know someone here?" I asked. His old nanny, I thought, and immediately endowed the woman with a history. She had raised Lord Paton from the egg, was dearer to him than his own mama, and he wished to present me to her. I felt a wave of emotion wash over me. Paton had not struck me as a sentimental man.

"I own the place," he said. "It was left to me by another aunt, who had bought it for the use of her retired companion. When the companion died, it was left idle. Let us go in and have a look around. Cozy, is it not?"

The puff of smoke from the chimney told me it was not vacant. The windows sparkled, and the rose-bushes had not returned to the wild. Someone was living here, some old family retainer probably. Lord Paton hopped down, secured the carriage, and came to assist me. I am neither old nor infirm. A hand would have been sufficient to see me safely to the ground, but it was two arms that lifted me down, making a fine flourishing circle with my body in the air before my feet reached terra firma. The unexpected trick threw me off balance, and I clutched at his shoulders for dear life, ready to deliver a sharp rebuke. But when I looked down at his jaunting, laughing face, my frown changed to a smile.

His hands remained at my waist after I released my grip on him. Then he removed one hand and put a finger under my chin, tilting my head up. "You don't look like a misogynist, Miss Nesbitt. Why do you write such cruel things about men? I cannot believe any man has had the heart to abuse such a lovely lady." His voice was burred with emotion as he gazed at me.

I lost track of time in the concentration of that speaking gaze. We just looked at each other for a long moment, then I took his arm and said calmly, "Let us go inside, Lord Paton. I'm freezing."

He was all solicitude, cursing himself as an insensitive monster. "We'll have a nice cup of tea—no, coffee is more fortifying. We'll pull our chairs close to the grate and make toast on the embers, as we used to do in the nursery. And don't you think we could dispense with the 'Lord,' Miss Nesbitt?"

Paton (you will notice I was not tardy to follow his advice) entered without knocking. A country housekeeper covered from neck to slippers in a white apron came trotting up. I waited to see who else came to greet us.

"Coffee, Mrs. Maherne, if you please. And see that the fire is built up."

"It's roaring away. Everything is in order, just as

you asked," she replied, and went off to make the coffee.

I noticed that Paton had taken some pains to make this visit pleasant. He had notified Mrs. Maherne of our arrival, which showed some forethought. But why had we come here, if not to meet some family or friend?

He ushered me into the parlor, a cozy little nook with low ceiling, a horsehair sofa set against one wall, a shelf of books against the other, and the blazing grate. He drew two stuffed chairs close to it and made a great fuss about my comfort. Did I want a shawl? No, I would be fine by the grate. Damme, there was no shawl. A blanket, perhaps, to put around my shoulders? He must find a coat for me to use on the return trip.

"Is there no one else in the cottage except Mrs. Maherne?" I asked. "Perhaps I ought not to stay . . ."

"There is no need to fear for the proprieties. Mrs. Maherne is a perfectly honorable chaperone. She used to keep house for the vicar," he assured me.

When the coffee arrived, Paton settled down to watch my performance. I made sure to hold the pot a judicious foot above the cup, to show my confidence. It was not necessary to toast bread over the embers. Sandwiches and plum cake accompanied the coffee. The fire would not be fit for making toast for an hour in any case, for the flames leapt up the chimney in a way that raised a fear for the thatched roof.

We ate a few sandwiches and soon settled back with our coffee, gazing into the fire. "Why did you choose to come here, Paton?" I asked.

"I have been wanting to be with you like this,

alone, so that we might come to know each other," he explained.

"It is very cozy, is it not?"

"The cottage is untenanted at the moment," he said, and looked at me with brightly eager eyes. "Now, don't pour the scalding coffee on me, Miss Nesbitt, but I am going to make a suggestion that may surprise you. I would like you to live here. It is not a mansion, but it is better than that little space under the eaves where you presently reside. Autumn does not show the place to best advantage, but in spring and summer it is charming, with a little garden in the back."

"Live here? Oh, I could not. Thank you, Paton, but really, it is more than I could afford at present."

He looked thunderstruck. "Good God, I'm not trying to *rent* it! I want you to have the place, rent free, with the housekeeper thrown in."

It was my turn to be thunderstruck. "I couldn't accept such a favor. I hardly know you."

He grasped my hand and squeezed it. "That is easily remedied, Miss Nesbitt. We could begin by dispensing with the Miss. I don't even know your name," he said, and scowled at this absurdity.

"Emma."

"Emma Nesbitt," he said, trying it like a connoisseur savoring a vintage port. "It has a—friendly sound. May I call you Emma?"

"It is a little early for us to be . . ."

"But then, who will know?" he asked, and smiled intimately. "I doubt that Mrs. Speers will be scandalized. She calls Madame de Staël Anne Louise, on what I take to be a very minimal acquaintance."

79

"None actually, but it was Miss Potter I was think-ing of."

"A high stickler, is she?"

"Toplofty as the devil." I laughed. "But I can al-ways handle her. She scolds that it is my leaving home that accounts for my waywardness, and no doubt she is right. I little thought, when I left Nes-bitt Hall, that I would find myself at such a party as the one where we met, Paton."

"And to think, I very nearly went to a concert instead. Had the music been anything but another recital of Handel, we would not have met. Do you think fate is trying to tell us something?" he asked flirtatiously.

I tossed my shoulders impertinently. "I pay no heed to that tyrant. I mean to arrange my own fate, thank you."

"With a little help from myself, I hope. You will take the cottage?"

It was nothing new under the sun for a wealthy nobleman to sponsor the arts. What bothered me was that Paton was young and handsome, I a single lady. It was open to misconstruction. "You know very well I cannot, though it is kind of you to pa-tronize the arts in this way. We do not have a car-riage, you see, and would be stuck in the country," I added as a sop.

"My aunt has a chaise she never uses. We'll hire a team."

I gave him a saucy smile. "What did you have in mind?" It was the cream ponies I referred to.

Paton hesitated a moment, then decided not to recognize my hint. "A pair of bloods, in any shade you wish." There was a moment of embarrassing silence. "The cottage is not so very far from Bath. You notice we made the trip in an hour," he said, adroitly changing the subject.

"Let us settle this once and for all, Paton. I have not the least intention of accepting charity from you or anyone else."

"It is not charity! The place is standing idle."

"Then rent it to someone—someone other than me. I have no wish to live in the country."

He listened, and appeared sad but soon came up with another idea. "How about London? As you enjoy city life, you would like London better than Bath."

"Bath will do for the nonce. Why should I go to London?" I thought he must have an apartment or house available there too.

"Bath is an odd destination for a lady who has decided to defy convention. I would have thought London a likelier home for such a dasher as you, Emma."

"You may well ask why a carefully reared lady ran away from home to live in a hovel and earn her own livelihood in Bath! I was a little frightened to tackle London on my own, you see. I am a provincial spirit at heart, and Bath is less wicked. Also, Mr. Pepper produces his *Ladies' Journal* there."

He nodded. "I'm glad you chose Bath. I gather from your writing that the situation at home was intolerable. You are obviously not a lady to be hampered by convention."

"You really did read my essay, then?"

"Carefully. I was shocked. Is it all true?"

"Every word."

"It seems incredible that a father would be so hard on his only daughter," he said, shaking his head.

"He had been reading *Émile*," I replied through thin lips.

"That accounts for your snipe at Rousseau the evening we met. I hope you do not leap from the specific to the general. Not all gentlemen are bounders."

"I did not say so, or imply it. I wrote only of my own plight, and my own solution. I would not like to give the impression I am an anarchist," I added. "Mr. Pepper feels I am the logical successor to Mary Wollstonecraft."

"I assumed she was your inspiration. It is unfortunate that no one took up the torch she lit. She and her husband, William Godwin, like you, totally rejected Rousseau's 'Contract Theory.' "

"Yes, of course," I said vaguely. I had seen something called *Du Contrat Social* in the library at home, and would have felt on firmer ground if I had read it.

"Tell me, as a disenfranchised and discontented young lady, which of Godwin's four bugbears concerns you more? Do you agree with him on all four points?"

Paton was obviously not talking about north, south, east, and west. I was slipping into deep and dangerous water here. I knew only that my newfound heroine, Mary Wollstonecraft, had married William Godwin, a dissenting minister. What could the question mean? "I seldom agree with Rousseau on anything," I said evasively. "That tends to put me in Godwin's camp, I suppose."

"Yet strangely enough, Mary Wollstonecraft

urged ladies to acquire that same education that Godwin despised for men."

Education was one of the four points, then. I latched on to it for dear life. "Oh, not the same education, surely. Merely to develop the mind for its job in life. An illiterate wife makes a sorry life's companion. And in any case, I am not totally familiar with Godwin's views," I admitted.

"He claims that between the four of them: the educational system, the government, religion, and the social order, society makes unthinking slaves of men. He would have every man a rational man, choosing his own morality."

"Good gracious, he sounds a dangerous fellow. I wonder the government didn't clamp him in irons. I dare say he was against paying his taxes. That should have made a good pretext for incarceration."

"He had some powerful allies. But really, it is more your philosophy on the social order and religion that I am interested to hear."

"Oh, I don't write philosophy. I don't want to be too clever for anyone to understand me."

"Perhaps you underestimate your audience's intelligence. In any case, I wish you would tell me about it. I would like to try to understand how you think."

This philosophical sort of conversation was totally new to me, and interesting. It was the kind of discussion I had hoped to encounter at that literary soirée. "So far as religion goes, I am a Christian, Paton. Wanting some equality with men does not make me a witch, you know. If it is the social contract that gives men all the influence and money, then I am against that."

"What do you mean by a Christian?"

I frowned in perplexity. "What everyone else means. I believe in Christ, and the tenets of Christianity, the Ten Commandments. I do not believe in killing or stealing. Just what sort of farouche creature do you take me for, that you are asking these questions?"

The only possibility I could think of was that he feared I was too outré to present to his friends and family. Perhaps he feared that I would go around pressing them not to pay their taxes, or skip church on Sunday.

"Godwin did not believe in the sacraments—baptism, marriage, and so on," he said. The curious way he looked at me seemed to anticipate an earth-shattering view.

"That is news to me. He married Mary Wollstonecraft. She had enough education to insist upon it, you see. Had she been as ignorant as men would like, Godwin would probably have tried his hand at seducing her."

"She permitted herself to be seduced, despite her education," he parried with a brightly curious smile. "It was the coming arrival of a child that precipitated the marriage."

I blushed like a blue cow. "Then they can neither of them have had the courage of their convictions—fortunately for the child. You seem very well informed on this couple, Paton. Were you one of Godwin's freethinkers?"

"He engaged my heart, to some extent, but not my mind. I dislike jail, and always make a point to pay my taxes. That is not to say I can't understand another's point of view. I succumbed to a university education without complaint, and even took some pleasure from it. I support the church," he added vaguely.

"Then you may be acquitted of Godwin's four heresies, for you go along with the church, the universities, and by implication, the government."

"That is only three," he pointed out.

"I know you would never be caught out in a social indiscretion." This deep conversation left me little time for tangential thoughts, such as Angelina.

Paton's conscious expression and arch smile alerted me what he was thinking, though he did not come right out and admit his scarlet life. "A bachelor is granted a wide degree of latitude without incurring society's wrath," he said.

It stung like a nettle, and I decided to give him a notion of my feelings on the matter. "Yes, a bachelor's improprieties are tolerated, but let a spinster go an inch out of line and she is ruined forever, cast into the abyss."

He gave me a searching look. "We are speaking of sexual improprities, I take it?"

My cheeks flushed at such broad talk, and I said vaguely, "Well—yes, in part." He nodded warmly. "Not that I mean to say I have run amok in that respect!"

"No, no! We are speaking generalities only. It is true men do judge more harshly in such matters. Ladies, unlike gentlemen, are expected to be perfectly innocent before marriage. Those who have stumbled can expect love and cherishing, but not a gold ring. It is unfair, but a fact." He examined me closely. I felt an apology in his look, an apology for Angelina, and rushed on to reassure him that I was as capable of forgiveness as anyone.

"So long as a man's diversions cease with marriage, a lady in love, being temporarily insane, will usually forgive his past," I said encouragingly.

Something in my speech made him uncomfortable. I don't know what it was, for I felt I had been generous in my view, but the cozy atmosphere cooled noticeably. Paton continued perfectly polite, but no longer warm.

"More coffee?" I suggested, lifting the pot with gracefully curved wrist.

Paton pulled out his watch. "We had best be getting you home, Miss Nesbitt, before darkness falls."

I stared in surprise and dismay. Surely it was a slip of the tongue that had lowered me back to Miss Nesbitt. Our outing had already lasted a long time though, and we still had the drive home to accomplish.

"Yes indeed. Miss Potter will be wondering what happened to me."

"I'll just have a word with the housekeeper," he said, and disappeared into the kitchen, to return a moment later with his curled beaver already in place. "All set?"

There was no mention of a coat or blanket for me, and in the new air of constraint around us, I did not like to remind him. We went out into a cruelly punishing wind. Paton's concern was all for his nags.

"I should have brought a blanket, as there's no stable here. I hope this pair of bloods haven't taken a chill."

He patted their flanks a moment, then lent me his

hand for the ascent, but in a detached way, as though I were a maiden aunt. He hopped aboard himself, whipped up the horses, and we were off. The force of the wind was felt more keenly as we drove into it. If I didn't come down with pneumonia, I would feel fortunate.

It was just as we pulled into Corsham that the leaden clouds began to spit down a desultory, cold rain.

"That's all we needed," he said grimly.

You would think we had spent an afternoon amongst savage Indians, or on the rack. Driving an open carriage to a miserable cottage in the country had not been my idea.

My patience broke, and I said, "You had best pull into the inn, or we'll catch our death of cold. I'm frozen to the bone already."

"It's a pity you hadn't worn a pelisse," he murmured.

"If I had known you meant to drive an open carriage and travel out into the wilds, I would have."

"I'm terribly sorry, Miss Nesbitt. That was thoughtless of me. I'll stop and give you my coat, till we reach the inn, and rest there till this rain lets up."

"Don't bother stopping. We're almost there."

"If you say so." At the driveway he slowed the team and turned in.

To give him an inkling of my feelings, I said ironically, "A perfect ending to a perfect afternoon. It remains only for the place to be crowded to the rafters so that we cannot hire a chamber."

He drew to a stop and turned to examine me. Words fail to describe the way Paton looked when I made that curt speech. Shock comes to mind. But if he was shocked at my sudden outbreak into rudeness, it should have been followed by annoyance. There was no annoyance to be seen. Interest gleamed in his dark eyes, curiosity certainly, all of it ending in a small, hopeful smile.

"Oh, I'm sure the proprietor can find us a chamber," he said with some slight emphasis on the last word.

"I mean a parlor, naturally."

His eyes narrowed and he said, "Naturally." I could not read his expression as he hopped down.

Chapter Eight

A GROOM GRABBED the reins, Paton took hold of my elbow, and we covered the distance from curricle to inn door at a speed to rival Paton's team. As soon as we were inside we saw that we were not the only travelers seeking shelter from the shower. Half a dozen farmers and itinerant pedlars stood about the timbered lobby, talking. One of the latter had brought his pack of toys in and was showing his wares to the others. From the tap room there came the sound of muted, afternoon revelry.

"I'll see to a parlor," Paton said, and strode to the desk.

He spoke to the clerk, the clerk's head shook in a negative way, and I realized we were destined to wait out the shower in the public lobby. It was only an inconvenience, not a tragedy, for the shower was light and we would soon be on our way. A nice hot cup of tea would have been welcome to dispel the chill caused by damp shoulders, however.

Paton returned and said, "The clerk tells me all the parlors are filled."

"I was afraid so. We shall just wait till the rain lets up and continue on our way."

He looked at the shoulders of my suit, where raindrops had darkened the blue to navy. "There is a bedchamber available, if you wish to sit by a fire for a half hour and warm up."

A vague feeling of dis-ease had been gathering over the last moments. It even occurred to me that Paton had something dishonorable in mind. "Oh, no! That would not be at all the thing!" I exclaimed. I would sooner catch pneumonia, though I did not say so.

"I thought perhaps a nice hot cup of tea," he said. "I would await you in the tap room."

My hackles calmed at this bland speech. "Could we not have it here, standing by the desk?" I suggested.

A superior sort of female servant, dressed all in black, was hurrying toward us. I had no idea who she might be and paid little heed till she stopped dead in front of me. "I beg your pardon, ma'am," she said very civilly. "Lady DeGrue saw you arrive and feared you were stranded, as she has taken the last parlor. She wishes me to invite you and your friend to join her."

It was a gift from the gods, and I jumped on it. "How very kind! We shall be delighted." I smiled and turned to Paton.

His surprise was evident, but he did not share my delight. His dark eyes wore a frustrated glitter. "Most kind," he said, and with a hand on my elbow led me off after the servant. "I didn't realize you were acquainted with Lady DeGrue."

"You know her too?"

"She is a friend of my aunt's," he explained.

The first thing I noticed upon entering the chamber was the welcoming warmth. A fire roared at the grate, casting an orange light on Lady DeGrue and her charge, Miss Bonham. They sat at a round table with a pot of tea and a plate of bread and butter in front of them. Lady DeGrue wore an enormous feathered bonnet, a lace fichu not unlike my own, and a woolen shawl wrapped around her shoulders. Her niece looked much less grand in a plain gown and round bonnet. She looked pale and subdued, as she had the other evening at the Upper Rooms. I noticed her mien brightened somewhat when she looked at Lord Paton. She had an eye for the gentlemen, then, despite her prissy ways.

Lady DeGrue said to her servant, "Two more cups, Waxon, and we shall require more hot water." Then she nodded severely at myself and Paton. "Miss Nesbitt, Paton."

I curtsied, he bowed, the dame continued speaking. "I spotted you darting in from your rig. A pity you were caught in the rain. You ought to know better than to take a lady out in an open carriage in this season, Paton. Set Miss Nesbitt by the fire, Isabel."

"So very kind of you," I said.

Miss Bonham rose and smiled vaguely halfway between Paton and myself. I drew a chair as close to the fire as Lady DeGrue's chair permitted. She was backed against it and soaked up most of its warmth. The room was so small, however, that it heated the entire space with no difficulty.

While we waited for the cups to arrive, Lady DeGrue gave Paton a lecture on the folly of driving an open rig. "I am surprised you were lured into believing a blue sky meant no rain," she said. "I never permit Miss Bonham to drive in an open rig. Of course, she is delicate. Your Miss Nesbitt is a sturdier gel."

"How very wise of you," Paton replied.

"You don't reach my age without being wise. I have seen a good many ladies put into the ground due to a dowsing. And you were not even wearing a mantelet, Miss Nesbitt," she added condemningly over her shoulder.

Miss Bonham smiled apologetically and said, "You are returning to Bath now, Miss Nesbitt?"

"Yes, as soon as the rain lets up, we shall be on our way."

"We have been visiting friends at Corsham Court," she said.

"Lord Methuen." I nodded.

"Oh, you know Methuen?"

"I have not met him. Paton mentioned him this afternoon."

"We all chose an ill day for a little jaunt."

I had the feeling Miss Bonham was fishing for an explanation of what lured me out in such weather. Her aunt was less devious. I heard her demand of Paton, "Where were you and Miss Nesbitt, if you don't mind my asking?" but I did not hear his reply.

Miss Bonham was saying, "Have you known Paton very long? I noticed he rushed to join your set at the ball the other evening. Is that where you met?"

"No, I knew him before that. We met at a party in Bath earlier."

"You were not acquainted before coming to Bath?"

"No. Have you known Paton long?"

"Long, but not well," she said. "We first met him in London some years ago. His aunt in Bath, Lady Forrest, is some connection to Lady DeGrue, not related, but only connected."

The water and cups arrived. It was very warm by the fire. My shoulders were not only dried but beginning to scorch. I removed to the table before I should be kippered alive. Lady DeGrue, with vast confidence but weak wrists, lifted the water jug only to the rim of the teapot and poured a great deal of water into the pot without adding any tea. She motioned to Miss Bonham, who did the pouring in a very ladylike way. It was not her fault that the liquid coming from the spout was very little darker than when it went in. It was hot at least, and accepted gratefully. Lady DeGrue took the last slice of bread and butter herself and proceeded to devour it.

"What a wretched tea," she complained when she had finished.

One did not like to say that the inn no doubt had tastier fare than bread and butter and watered tea. "But what can one expect." She shrugged. "Waxon," she called toward the corner. "I believe I saw a pedlar in the lobby. See what he is selling. If it is anything I would be interested in, bring him to me. And make sure you shut the door behind you. There is a wretched draft in here." The place felt like an oven.

Waxon left. During her brief absence the dame quizzed Paton about a number of people whose names I did not recognize and asked me where Miss Potter was today.

"She is at home," I said.

Waxon apparently found the pedlar's wares of interest to her employer, for she led him in. He was a round-shouldered old fellow, dressed in dusty fustian. A certain aroma accompanied him.

"Put your sack here on the table where I can see it," Lady DeGrue ordered.

A dirty leather pouch was set on the table amidst the teacups, and the man began to draw out his goods. Needles and threads, buttons and lace and ribbons were his wares.

"Tuppence for a packet of needles! You're mad. I'll give you a farthing for them," she asserted.

"Oh, milady. You jest," he said, showing a set of pink gums with a few shattered teeth. "I could sell you one needle for a farthing if you have urgent need of it."

"Idiot. What urgent need would I have for a needle? Your threads, then. That blue just matches your muslin, Isabel. Its seams could do with reinforcing. I don't know how you manage to tear all your gowns apart. That blue muslin is not three years old, and already the seams are coming loose."

"Tuppence," the pedlar said.

He was castigated for a thief and a knave, and offered two farthings. The poor man was made to empty his pack item by item, receiving a dozen insults on the shoddiness of his merchandise and the inordinate prices he was asking. And after all that, Lady DeGrue did not purchase so much as a needle or box of pins. I was happy to see Paton slipped a coin into the man's hand as he left.

When this performance was over, Lady DeGrue drew her shawls more tightly around her and picked up her reticule. "Well, that helped to pass a very dull stop," she said. This oblique comment on our company was no doubt unintentional. "A pity he smelled like a barn. I hope he buys himself a bath with that coin you gave him, Paton. You don't want to encourage such creatures as that. Take a look out the window, Waxon, and see if the rain has stopped."

Waxon duly reported that it was nearly let up.

"Still spitting, is it?" Lady DeGrue said, and strode to the window, where a weak and watery sun was trying to fight through the clouds. "There is nothing else for it, Miss Nesbitt. You will have to come home in my closed carriage."

Paton glanced at the window and said, "The rain has stopped."

"It will start again e'er long," Lady DeGrue informed him. "You will not want to expose Miss Nesbitt to such weather. Next time take your closed carriage, and you should have worn a pelisse, Miss Nesbitt. There is no point defying the weather. Miss Potter would never forgive me, nor would I forgive myself, if you took a chill. No need to thank me, Paton," she said, turning to my escort. "I know you will insist on paying for tea. You bucks are all alike, so thoughtful. Come along, Isabel. Miss Nesbitt, do you want a corner of my shawl?"

I declined the shawl, but was not ungrateful for the drive in the closed carriage.

Lady DeGrue looked closely from Paton to myself and said, "You two will want a moment's privacy to arrange your next meeting. We shall be in the lobby. Do not keep us waiting long, Miss Nesbitt. My niece has weak lungs."

The party swept out with a fine flurry of shawls and I turned to Paton. "Nosy old biddybody," he scowled.

"I shall go with her all the same. I should have

worn a pelisse. Thank you for the outing. It was—interesting."

He bowed gracefully. "It was my pleasure. Thank you for obliging me."

No attempt was made to arrange our next meeting. I joined Lady DeGrue at a speed that not even that high stickler found fault with. We went to the carriage. It was soon clear that the ladies had compared notes during the moment I was absent. As soon as the door was closed, Lady DeGrue began a quizzing.

"Isabel tells me Paton is a fairly new acquaintance, Miss Nesbitt. You have known him only since arriving in Bath?"

"Yes, for a few weeks now."

"He is an excellent parti, of course, very high in the stirrups, and comes from good stock. I congratulate you. I dare say you never expected to nab a duke's son."

"I do not expect to nab Paton," I said.

"Very proper. Till he asks you, you must not express the notion that he is caught in Parson's mousetrap. Nothing is likelier to make a man turn tail and run."

"No, truly! We are just friends."

"Ho, sly minx! As if a well-bred young lady like yourself would go jauntering around the countryside on no more surety than that." Her calculating glance turned to Isabel. "That is how a lady nabs a gentleman, Isabel. You are too backward. You scarcely said boo to Paton at dinner last week, and here he was ripe for the plucking. We must make a harder push to find you a parti. I cannot go rattling about to balls and routs forever."

96

Isabel cast a shy smile at me.

I wanted to dispel the idea that Paton and I were close friends and said, "It happened Lord Paton had to look into a small property nearby that he has inherited. He invited me to accompany him on the drive."

"That would be Angelina's lovenest." Lady De-Grue nodded blandly. "The little Tudor cottage with roses at the door?"

Apparently Lady DeGrue found nothing amiss with this outing. I was shocked, and did not bother to conceal it.

"Did you not know?" she asked, nose quivering for news.

"The subject did not arise."

"He has turned her off, never fear. We were all wondering whether he has found a new light o' love, or had decided to marry. His papa, the dear duke, has been at him this age to settle down. He would like to see a grandson before he sticks his fork in the wall. There is no word of a new lightskirt, and as he and you are so famously close . . ."

Further protestations proved vain. She had decided I was Paton's betrothed, and as it was clear that was the only reason she had befriended me, I protested no more. But the awful idea was forming that he had taken me to Angelina's lovenest for a quite different reason.

"Paton is making a mighty long stay in Bath. Now we know why," she finished archly.

"He is attending to some properties for his aunt. They are building a set of apartments," I informed her.

"That will be more gold lining for his pockets before long. His aunt is seventy if she's a day. I was still making the rounds when she made her bows. You must come to call on Isabel one day," she declared as we approached Bath.

Though hardly ideal, Lady DeGrue and Miss Bonham were the first respectable acquaintances I had made in Bath, and I expressed mild pleasure at this notion.

We returned by a different route than Paton had taken out of the city. We had descended well into the heart of town before I realized it. "I think we have passed my house," I exclaimed when I noticed the error.

"Where do you live?" Lady DeGrue asked. Her niece, though a fully mature lady at least as old as myself, seldom spoke until spoken to.

"On Lampards Street."

"Ah, way up on top of the hill. My poor nags will never make it. I take this circuitous path to avoid the steeper inclines. You should move closer to the heart of the city, Miss Nesbitt. It will be best if we let you off on Milsom Street, where you can easily hire a cab. Give Isabel your address before you leave, and we will drop you a note to let you know when you may call on us."

A grim, yellow-toothed smile accompanied this piece of condescension. Not eager to display my inferior abode, I kept my tongue between my teeth and thanked Lady DeGrue before leaving her carriage. She sent Waxon to find me a cab, then I was let down.

During the steep haul up the downs, I reviewed my afternoon outing. It had begun well enough, but overall I was not happy with it. The destination, upon consideration, seemed extraordinarily inappropriate. It was bizarre that Paton offered me a cottage rent free. I had first taken it for a nobleman's patronage to an aspiring writer. But for a bachelor to offer it to a spinster—that added a new flavor, one that I found bitter.

Was I imagining that it was his intention to replace Angelina with me? Surely to God he did not take me for such a depraved creature! Yet we had met under less than auspicious circumstances at a party where Annie and I were, in fact, the only real ladies in the room. And I had hardly looked the part in that idiotic turban that kept falling askew. With Mrs. Speers's uncertainty over my name, he had taken me for a dashing divorcée. When I considered that he knew I should have been in mourning for a recently deceased father, my shame was complete.

Reviewed in this new light, I realized that during the visit the conversation had taken some highly questionable turns. All that talk of fallen women and the impossibility of their finding a husband. "Godwin did not believe in the sacraments— baptism, marriage . . ." Of course I had loudly and instinctively expressed my outrage. And very shortly after, Paton had lost all interest in me.

The wretch had taken me to Angelina's cottage to try his hand at seducing me. A cottage, with a housekeeper and a carriage thrown in, all the perquisites usually bestowed on a man's mistress. Including a little lovenest discreetly removed from town. He took me for a lightskirt! No other conclusion was possible.

I was ready to burst with annoyance. Even at the inn at Corsham he still hoped to seduce me. It was a room he was after, a bedchamber, not a parlor. I thanked my old opponent, Fate, for having sent Lady DeGrue to forestall any more unpleasantness. Her friendship must have convinced Paton that I was thoroughly respectable, barring my abode and lack of mourning. He had no way of knowing how superficial was the acquaintance.

And now, if I judged Lady DeGrue accurately, she would be whispering to her crones that Miss Nesbitt had caught Lord Paton. It would not be long before the rumor found its way back to him. I felt helpless to prevent this comical disaster. There was nothing I could do. And really, it served Paton right. My humor was restored by the time the carriage reached Lampards Street.

"Did you have a nice outing?" Annie asked eagerly.

"It was different," I assured her. Should I tell Annie? She read me enough lectures without handing her that extra fuel on a platter. I made much of having met Lady DeGrue, and very little of Angelina's cottage.

"Will he be calling again?" she asked.

"Perhaps. He did not mention a specific day or time. And what have you been doing all afternoon, Annie?"

Arthur had been to call. A recital of his various utterances passed the time till dinner, and in the evening, he was to take us to a concert. I wondered if Lord Paton would be in attendance.

Chapter Nine

HAD I BEEN asked to name the three people I wished least to encounter that evening, it would have been Lord Paton, Geoffrey Nesbitt, and Lady DeGrue, in that order. Fate repaid me for her afternoon's defeat by casting two of the three into my path at the concert. To make up for the lack of Cousin Geoffrey, she threw in a substitute in the person of Lady Forrest, Paton's septuagenarian aunt. The concert itself was bad enough, consisting as it did of an Italian tenor singing madrigals, accompanied by the violin. The only relief from this was a few of Mozart's louder works pounded out on the pianoforte by a gentleman with two wooden hands and a tin ear. I was in the mood for a set of waltzes, or some light play music, perhaps from *The Beggar's Opera*.

"Shall we slip out while the slipping is good?" Pepper suggested at the intermission.

Having paid the penalty, I was strongly inclined to grasp the reward and mix with the throng for tea. That is where the mischief occurred. We were no sooner at a table than Lady DeGrue and Miss Bonham landed in on us. She has more than one trick to get her tea without expense. I later learned her most common one is to wait till she sees an acquaintance with the tea already laid, then she sits down uninvited and takes her refreshment gratis.

"Miss Nesbitt!" she hollered across the room. "And Miss Potter. No need to thank me for delivering your charge home safe and sound." She smiled at Annie. "I was delighted to do it for you."

It was news to me that I resided on Milsom Street, but I had to pretend to be grateful. Annie asked, "Who the devil is that?" but as soon as I reminded her, she said all that was proper. By that time Lady DeGrue and Miss Bonham had slid onto the extra chairs. The latter looked apologetic, the former examined Pepper through her lorgnette and apparently did not count on his having the manners to invite her to take tea. She collared a servant and demanded more cups herself. "And a fresh pot, mind. We don't want to drink hot water." She turned back to Annie. "There is no counting on them to have the wits to bring a fresh pot. Miss Nesbitt will tell you what a paltry tea Paton served us this afternoon." She turned her lorgnette in my direction. "And where is Paton this evening? Slipped the leash, has he, sly dog?"

"I have no i—" She had been scanning the room and found him. "Ah, there he is with Agatha. He has dragged his poor aunt out for a night's frolic. With her gouty knees, she ought to be allowed to stay home. I see how it is." She smiled archly at me. "He could not stay away from you, Miss Nesbitt."

My first reaction was dismay to hear Paton was present. It seemed extremely unlikely that he had dragged his aunt out to such an antique frolic as this. It must have been she who had done the dragging, but in either case, it had nothing to do with me. No matter, before anyone could stop her, Lady DeGrue raised her hand and bellowed to them. "Agatha. Yoo-hoo, Agatha." Then aside to me: "She is deaf as a bat, poor soul. Right here, Paton," she called louder. "There is an empty table beside Miss Nesbitt."

I looked at Lady Forrest, because I did not wish to look at her nephew. She was of a different stamp altogether from Lady DeGrue, a fat, jolly-looking lady, wearing a mauve gown, rouge, and a great many jewels. I saw her make some derogatory comment to Paton, but in the end, tables were in short enough supply that they legged it to the empty one beside us. They stopped for a few words, and it was no longer possible to avoid looking at Paton. It would take a deal of imagination to see any vestige of admiration on his impassive face. He bowed, and showed exactly the same degree of pleasure to see me as to see Annie and Pepper, or the table, which is to say a very minimal amount, if any.

"I am happy to see you have not come down with a chill, Miss Nesbitt," he said.

"Thanks to Lady DeGrue, I am fine." I had not meant to sound so ingracious to Lord Paton in front of company. In the unlikely event that I was ever again alone with this man, it would be a different story, but in society I meant to remain ignorant of his former intentions.

"Regrettable weather we ran into," he murmured.

His aunt examined me with a pair of sharp blue eyes, undimmed by her age. There was no malice in her regard, which told me she knew nothing of her nephew's doings. She seemed curious, no more. I expect the fact that Lady DeGrue was with us colored me pure and dull. She and Paton sat at their table and fell into some private conversation.

Lady DeGrue never believed in being private, or allowing anyone else that luxury. The larger audience she could muster, the better. "I say, Agatha," she called, "Miss Nesbitt tells me you are building some apartments."

I squirmed under Lady Forrest's astonished stare. Paton glared. I shrank visibly. Pepper regarded us all and smiled his puckish smile.

"It is on that parcel of land adjacent to Brandon Hill, is it, or Tyndalls Park?" Lady DeGrue shouted. Lady Forrest made some inaudible reply. "A nasty cold wind your tenants will get, but you need not bother your head about that," Lady DeGrue said.

She put three quarters of the cakes on her own plate and carried the plate and her cup over to Lady Forrest's table without even saying good-bye or thank you. Miss Bonham smiled her customary apologetic smile. I felt sorry for the girl, and passed her what remained of the cakes. She refused, to make up for her aunt's piggishness.

"My aunt told me to ask you to a drum on Saturday evening, Miss Nesbitt," she said shyly. "And Lord Paton, of course. She will be sending cards, but perhaps you will tell me now whether you are free."

Only in Bath would a route still be called a drum! "I am free, and would be delighted to attend. I cannot be sponsor for Lord Paton's attendance, however."

"But you and your chaperone will come?" She

seemed eager for my acquaintance. The girl was exquisitely dull, but rather pitiful. Her aunt must run her a wretched life.

"We will be very happy to."

"I am so glad. Perhaps we could drive out some afternoon you are not seeing Lord Paton."

"My afternoons are quite free," I assured her.

"Auntie does not like me to go out alone, and she is not much for driving about without a reason. Waxon accompanies me at times, but she is really my aunt's companion. Shall we say—tomorrow afternoon, if you are not busy, that is."

"That would be lovely, Miss Bonham."

"I shall call for you at Lampards Street." As this was said in a low voice, I understood Miss Bonham meant to deceive her aunt, the wicked girl. There was hope for her yet. "The team are really very sturdy," she explained, again apologetically.

"I expect you have many friends in Bath, as you make your home here?" This was a cunning and unworthy trick on my part. I had a pretty good idea she was friendless, and she soon confirmed it.

"My aunt is very strict about whom she allows me to see. Any friend of Paton, of course, must be unexceptionable."

I smiled demurely. "Perhaps we could go to the Pump Room. My chaperone will be happy to come with us," I added swiftly when her eyebrows drew together in doubt at such rakishness.

Her beaming smile showed her appreciation. "Or for a stroll in the Crescent Gardens, as we will be suitably chaperoned."

We had a nice girlish chat after that. The "girlish" refers to Miss Bonham more than to myself. Although beyond girlhood in years, it was clear she was lacking in polish. The extent of her wickedness was driving and walking. She suggested the circulating library as another pastime, and I mentioned visiting the shops.

Thus passed the tea break. By keeping up a constant guard, I refrained from looking at the adjacent table. Any glimpses accomplished from the corner of my eye convinced me that Paton was not paying me any heed. When tea was over, the two groups rose and stood together a moment. Lady DeGrue studied the program. "More Mozart. How I look forward to that," she said. Miss Bonham smiled submissively, and they returned to the concert.

Lady Forrest turned a sapient eye on me. I had no idea what Lady DeGrue had been saying, but it was soon clear that she had given the idea that Paton and I were on close terms. "We must get together for a chat soon, Miss Nesbitt," she said with an assessing smile. "As you appear to be quite familiar with me, I am curious to know you better. You must call on me."

I felt extremely foolish. "Lord Paton mentioned your building the apartments. I hope it is not a secret."

"Nothing is kept secret long in this town," she replied with an arch look from Paton to myself. I wished the floor would open up and swallow me. "I have had enough caterwauling for one evening, sonnie. How about you?"

Paton gave a conscious look at being addressed in this youthful fashion, but agreed he had enjoyed enough music.

"We are about to leave as well," Annie said, and we all gathered up our bits and pieces to leave.

The older group went ahead, with Paton and myself trailing uncomfortably behind. I felt an instinct to apologize for having told Lady DeGrue about his aunt's building plans. A second thought deterred me. He had more to apologize for, and if he said nothing, I would not mention the solecism.

"Did you enjoy the concert, Lord Paton?" I asked, purposely using the formal address.

He avoided calling me anything, and said, "It is not my own favorite sort of music. My aunt occasionally likes an evening out."

"I dare say she spends most of her time at home, at her age, although she seems spry enough."

"She prefers to have company visit her."

"Yes."

Not a syllable about Lady Forrest's invitation for me to call. I noticed his step was lagging, and wondered at it. "About this afternoon, Miss Nesbitt . . ." he said. A slight flush crept up his neck.

"Yes?" I gave a bright, inconsequential smile, determined not to reveal anything. Let him think I was ignorant of his intentions. It was the least embarrassing course to take, and one that might allow us to meet without either of us having to blush. And since I was eager to enlarge my circle of respectable friends, no invitation would be declined. I would visit Lady Forrest if she set a date. She was a local; she probably knew everyone. Lord Paton would not be long with her, but I planned to live here permanently.

His blush faded. Relief was written on every line

of his handsome face. Soon he broke into quite a natural smile. "It was unfortunate about the weather," he said.

I played along with him. "Indeed it was. You must have wondered that I was so eager to pitch myself into Lady DeGrue's carriage, but to tell the truth, I was freezing. I would have worn a pelisse had I known you meant to drive an open carriage."

"I should have told you! I usually keep a wrap in my curricle, but it happens it got muddied last week, and is being cleaned. Did you have a wretched drive home?"

"Not at all." Nothing was said of having been dropped off at Milsom Street. "Miss Bonham is better company than her aunt, you must know."

"Ah, you are a friend of Isabel's."

This misconception was not disturbed. It was a tricky business, accepting Paton's friendship as he thought me close to Lady DeGrue, and vice versa. If they ever got together and compared notes, I would be revealed as a vixen of the first water. "We have been laying all sorts of plans to rush around Bath, buying up bonnets and ogling the gentlemen on the Crescent," I said airily.

He smiled very nicely. It was different from the smile that quizzed me about Godwin and Rousseau. It was a smile reserved for *ladies,* and something inside me still stung to remember that afternoon.

"Isabel needs a friend like you. She is kept under a cat's paw. It is very kind of you to befriend her," he said.

I noticed that, although I was no longer considered

a lightskirt, I was still held to be more dashing than Miss Bonham. "I mean to bring her out of her shell, never fear."

"You are just the one who can accomplish it, Miss Nesbitt. I look forward to seeing you at Lady De-Grue's drum. You must not expect dancing, or even music, unless you or one of her guests are kind enough to oblige the party. Her drums are more muted than that."

My hopes for Saturday's entertainment diminished accordingly. This description was enough to make me wonder why Paton was attending. The two groups left with friendly au revoirs.

The remainder of the week passed comfortably. The writing was going well. Miss Bonham proved more diverting once I got her away from her aunt. Lady DeGrue, Isabel confessed, was eager to see her bounced off, and was loosening the reins. We accomplished all the plans we had discussed, i.e., drove in the carriage, walked in Crescent Gardens, went to the circulating library, and visited the shops. I learned by a combination of clever questioning and deduction that Miss Bonham was quite a rich heiress. Her aunt, on the other hand, was poor as a church mouse. This being the case, I wondered that Miss Bonham did not exert her will more forcibly. I had rather thought Miss Bonham kowtowed to her aunt to secure her fortune.

On her third visit, I purposely left her waiting half an hour while I dressed, and handed her a copy of *The Ladies' Journal* to peruse. It was my intention to open the door of independence to her at least a crack.

"Who writes such stuff?" she asked when we were installed in the carriage.

Annie coughed nervously, to warn me against revelation. "My landlady, for one," I said. "Do you not think there is something in it?"

"I have never had much to do with men," she confessed sadly. "I do not remember my papa at all. It seems to me that older ladies are the blight of most of our lives. They are the ones who won't let us do anything. Oh, I do not mean you, Miss Potter!" she added hastily.

I laughed gaily. "Good gracious, if I had your money, I would live like a queen. It is true older ladies can be quite as repressive as men if you let them. It is foolish to let anyone else lead your life for you. Your aunt has no authority to bearlead you. She is your dependent, not the other way around. You are twenty-five, and in control of your own fortune—till you marry that is."

"No one will ever marry me," she said dully.

"I should like to know why not! You are very pretty—isn't she pretty, Annie?"

"Pretty as a picture."

"You have a sweet temper, and you are as rich as Croesus," I added.

"I haven't the knack of attracting men."

"Shall we go to the shops today?" I suggested. "A fashionable new bonnet would be a good first step."

Miss Bonham looked remarkably better in a high poke bonnet with dashing feathers all around the band. Several heads turned as we strolled down Milsom Street, adding a few other elegant trifles to her wardrobe. She blossomed under the attention.

"I wish I could wear my new bonnet to Auntie's

drum tomorrow evening," she said just before she left us that day.

"You could wear a new hairdo. That would be equally effective," I pointed out. She had never changed her style from the first day I met her.

There was a new light in her eyes. They sparkled in a mischievous way that made her appear five years younger. "Perhaps I shall," she said, and laughed.

"Not 'perhaps'! *Do* it. Call Jean Leclair. He is the most sought after stylist coiffeur in Bath. You would look *ravissante* in a cherubim do. Would she not, Annie?"

"Where would I find him?" Isabel asked.

It was amazing to me that an heiress did not even know the best hairdresser in town. I gave her the address, and we waved Miss Bonham, whom we now called Isabel, off.

"I'll write this evening, to make up for all these outings," I said to Annie. "You can amuse yourself for a few hours, I dare say?"

"Arthur is dropping by," she replied.

Annie was making strides in her romance. Isabel was beginning to realize she had a life of her own. It occurred to me that everyone was bettering her position except myself. I had at least convinced Cousin Geoffrey that I was not returning. There had been no letters from him for some days. It was high time I looked about me for a beau. Perhaps the drum tomorrow evening would throw up someone.

While Pepper and Annie courted, I wrote on my novel. Before retiring, I caught up with my journal. When I began it, it was my intention to keep the tone high, dealing with the question of a lady's position in society circa 1817, but I was so fatigued that I found it sinking to a mere diary about my various outings that day, and my feelings toward Lord Paton. Still, an astute student might read something between the lines regarding a nobleman's character. It was a subject Hannah More had not found beneath her. Query: Are noblemen unscrupulous because of their wealth and position, or is a lack of scruples the way one acquires wealth and position?

Chapter Ten

I PREPARED MYSELF for Lady DeGrue's evening party with only moderate hopes that anything interesting would come of it. Paton's attending gave hope that he might bring some of his set, who would be considered the ton of sociable Bath. In an effort to win favor, I struck a rather pretty jeweled pin in the shape of a feather in my curls. The bronze taffeta gown that had set Milverton on its ear might still impress Bath. At any rate, I looked as good as a new hairdo, my best gown, and a discreet touch of rouge could make me. It was Annie who had bought the rouge—a great divergence from her usual toilette.

Miss Bonham lived, appropriately, on Quiet Street. The street is only one block long, its chief attraction being that it debouches on to Milsom Street, just a few blocks north of the Pump Room. The house was large but gloomy. The gloom was enlivened on the evening of the drum by lights in every window, and a scurry of carriages in the roadway.

I was happy to see, upon entering, that there was

a good crowd present, not all of it gray-haired. It seems an heiress, even if she has no town polish, can get out the bachelors. Isabel looked quite radiant with her sable curls now framing her face. I rather feared Lady DeGrue might take me to task for the transformation. It was no such a thing.

She got me aside early in the evening and said, "I can never thank you enough, Miss Nesbitt. You have contrived in a week what failed me for more than two decades. You have forced Isabel into bloom. It is a wonderful relief to me to know she is able to get about without my company, and still be well chaperoned. I shall hobble over and thank your Miss Potter."

Her gait was more a prance than a hobble, but she did go to Annie and said something that made her smile. The party gathered in a dark, brown-colored room which Lady DeGrue called the Gold Saloon, and spilled over into an adjoining room. There were forty or fifty people present, which created a pleasant buzz of voices. No sooner was I seated in the Gold Saloon than I discerned the younger set were in the other room. To rise up with no excuse and desert Reverend Morton in the middle of his monologue on the Trinity seemed rude, so I contented myself by just looking through the archway.

I was soon convinced that Paton, the one member of the young ton whom I knew, had not yet arrived. I had already had a word with Lady Forrest, and began to think Paton was not coming. The only reason I mention it, of course, is that I had thought he might bring his bachelor friends along. But at any rate, there were interesting men there, and Isabel had her share of them. She sat with a handsome specimen, dark of hair and eyes, with pale skin and the languid, wounded air of a poet. She gazed into his eyes dreamily, as if she were falling in love. A young maiden's first bout of love will often settle on some such handsome poseur as this gentleman.

After perhaps fifteen minutes, there was a shifting about of guests, and Lady Forrest, brilliant in diamonds and puce silk, beckoned me to a chair beside her.

"Miss Nesbitt, I took pity on you, stuck with old Morton. You can hear his sermon on the Trinity any Sunday at Holy Trinity Church. You must not waste a party in such tedious company. You ought to slip into the next room with the other youngsters. I wonder Miss Bonham does not arrange some dancing, since she has rooted out all the bachelors."

"Lord Paton tells me we must not expect either dancing or music, ma'am."

"No doubt that is why he is not here, the wretch. Where the devil is he tonight?"

I was astonished that she should ask me. I had not seen him since the concert. "I have no idea."

"You should keep closer track of him than that," she teased. "When are you coming to visit me, Miss Nesbitt?"

I found myself in the absurd position of apologizing for not honoring a nonexistent invitation, for I am not such a flat as to go calling on such a vague hint as I had received at the concert. "I have been spending a deal of time with Isabel," I explained.

"I can see the good effects of your company," she said, glancing into the other room. "You might just give her the hint that young Etherington is a gazetted fortune hunter."

"Is that the gentleman with her now?"

She seemed surprised that I did not know it. "Yes, Lord Ronald Etherington, a younger son of old Lord Britton. He owes every tradesman in London, and has had to retire to Bath to escape his creditors. It is public knowledge he is hanging out for a fortune. A word to the wise!"

"I shall warn Isabel."

Lady DeGrue strode into the next room to stir up the crowd. "Go to her now," Lady Forrest urged, and I went.

I arrived just as Lady DeGrue was distributing pieces of paper for some game. She had copied it out of a puzzle book, the object being for us to recognize in a set of clues a famous personage from history. We were to work in pairs, man and woman, to add a romantic spice.

Lord Ronald took a slip of paper and turned to speak to Isabel. Lady DeGrue forestalled him. "Sir Laurence is waiting for you, Isabel," she said.

Turning, I saw the elderly gentleman who had stood up with Isabel at the ball. Lady DeGrue presented him as Sir Laurence Edwards, a dear friend of the family. He was not elderly in the way Lady DeGrue was elderly. I judged him to be in his middle forties. He had quite a bit of gingery-colored hair, though it was thin at front. If the man had acted his age, he would have been a passable partner for one dance. What dismayed one about Sir Laurence was that he tried so desperately to look and act young. The dazzling yellow waistcoat belonged on a university student, as did the nip-waisted jacket and high shirt collars he wore with it. He capered, he talked and laughed loud. He used the cant terms of a young buck. One felt instinctively that he would drive too fast.

"Miss Bonham, you are stuck with me." He laughed, deepening the wrinkles along his nose. "We shall set them all on their ears, by Jove. What a charming new hairdo. You look like an angel. I have been calling on you all week to show off my new rattler and prads. It wears me to a thread to hold them down to sixteen miles an hour."

Isabel looked an apology over her shoulder, where Lord Ronald was sulking into his high collar.

"We shall drive out tomorrow, eh?" Sir Laurence persisted. "I'll teach you to handle the ribbons."

"Oh, I do not drive," she exclaimed in horror.

"High time you learned. All the crack. An out and outer like yourself ought to set up a high perch phaeton. Tell her, Miss Nesbitt."

"Miss Nesbitt, perhaps you would accompany Lord Ronald," Lady DeGrue suggested.

No sooner had I reluctantly accepted than Lord Paton strolled into the room. He looked all around, nodding to various people, including myself. I smiled coolly and turned to Lord Ronald.

"I despise childish games," he said.

I found one thing in common with Lord Ronald. "I fear there is to be no dancing," I mentioned.

"I despise dancing."

"Ah. Tell me, Lord Ronald, am I correct in thinking you might care for poetry?"

He gave me a bold, dismissing look, but a glint of interest lit his sultry eyes. "It depends on what you mean by poetry. I have no use for flowers nodding by a lake, or violets blooming unseen."

He was playing at being Byron then. "Corsairs and banditti are more your style, I take it?"

"At least they *live*. What foolishness have we to solve?" he sulked, and opened the paper. "Oh, God, it is history. Next to religion, it is the dullest thing they could have come up with."

I read the paper and decided Henry the Eighth was who we had to be. "This monarch was hardly dull," I said, and handed the paper back to him. "And we have not only to solve it, but feed clues to the others."

"My aversion to the Tudors is exceeded only by my loathing for the Hanovers," he said comprehensively.

"All things look yellow to the jaundiced eye," I snipped.

Lord Ronald gave me a bored look. His glance slid to Isabel. Were it not for her, he would have left the party, and I sincerely wished he would. She was looking at him hopefully, while Sir Laurence rattled on about some drinking spree he had enjoyed recently.

"Let us get this game over with." Lord Ronald scowled.

Isabel looked at Sir Laurence. "The older guests are going to play cards, Sir Laurence," she said temptingly.

"Good for them. It will keep them out of mischief. Let the rest of us get on with this game."

Defeated, she said, "First we have to put the chairs in a ring so that everyone can see and hear."

"If we are moving the chairs, why do we not dance?" Lord Ronald demanded.

"Do you not despise dancing, milord?" I asked.

His eyes smoldered in Isabel's direction. "That depends on one's partner."

"Very true. A surly partner can take the pleasure out of anything."

Isabel overheard his suggestion of dancing and undertook to apologize. "We did not hire any musicians, Lord Ronald," she said. "We can hardly dance without music."

He sensed a reprieve from the games, which were apparently even more despised than dancing, and said, "Surely someone can play the piano."

"It would disturb the card players," I said firmly.

"Oh, no," Isabel countered. "They do not play in the Gold Saloon. The card parlor is quite set off. If only someone could play the piano."

Annie used to perform this function at home, but I did not like to tear her away from Arthur. The solution came from a surprising direction.

"My aunt plays the piano. In fact, she would prefer it to cards," Lord Paton announced. "Would Lady DeGrue mind, Isabel?"

"Not if *you* asked her," she said artlessly, smiling from ear to ear.

He bowed. "It will be my pleasure."

I could not but compare the manners of Paton and Lord Ronald. Paton might be a womanizer, but at least he was one of pleasant disposition. And it was not their fortune he was after either. Rather than just complain, he undertook to correct an unpleasant evening. I found Lord Ronald a most disagreeable fop, despite his handsome face.

He earned full credit for persistence, however. By the time Lady Forrest sat down at the pianoforte, he had gotten Isabel's hand for the country dance that was forming, despite his loathing for dance. This left me partnerless, but not for long. Sir Laurence chose me, as Isabel's friend, and someone he could talk to about her.

All his youthful airs left him when he was not trying to impress Isabel. "I cannot imagine why Lady DeGrue invited Etherington here," he grouched. "The man has the reputation of a rake, just the sort of handsome, wellborn jackanapes to bowl Miss Bonham over. She is so innocent."

"We must drop her the clue he is not the thing."

"It will come better from you, Miss Nesbitt."

"Disparagement of a favored beau never comes well from anyone, but I shall tell her all the same."

I felt a little responsible, as I was the one who had cracked her shell. I doubted if Lord Ronald would have been bothered with Isabel, despite her fortune, if she had worn her old nunnish air.

It seemed the whole party was concerned over Isabel's quite obvious infatuation with Etherington. I noticed that Paton, too, was eyeing them askance, and as soon as the set was over, he went to claim her for the next dance. She looked one of her mute yet speaking apologies at me, and hurried Paton over to me as soon as the music stopped. I got hold of Sir Laurence's arm and nodded to Isabel. He was not tardy to claim her. He was no prize to be sure, but at least no one had condemned the man.

I assumed Lord Paton would ask me to stand up with him. He said, "It's warm in this small room. Shall we go next door and have a glass of orgeat, Miss Nesbitt?"

As Isabel was safely disposed for the next half

hour, I went along, curious to hear what he would have to say. His first words were, "Lord Ronald—"

"I know. I mean to tell her at the first opportunity."

He looked at me with amusement shining in his dark eyes. "I see there is no moss growing under *your* feet. What the devil is he doing here?"

"Despising everything except Lord Byron."

"A poor model he has chosen. Or are you one of the poet's followers?"

I gave him a pert smile. "Why is it you always suspect me of admiring the most outré personalities, Lord Paton? First William Godwin, now Lord Byron. I am not so debauched, I promise you."

"Very true. I apologize, Miss Nesbitt. Or should I say Emma? I seem to recall we had reached a first-name basis."

"Perhaps unadvisedly. Miss Nesbitt will do very well, Lord Paton. I dare say it was the nature of the outing, being caught in the rain and all, that caused us to fall into such quick intimacy."

He gave a disparaging smile. "Rain will often have that effect," he joked. "Had it been a snowstorm, we might have gone even farther, faster."

This remark was questionable enough, though unintentionally I think, that I decided to change the topic. "What literary works will you be featuring in the next issue of the *Quarterly*?"

"I am doing something on a fellow called Shelley. Do you still continue with your essays, Miss Nesbitt? I do not hear anyone speak to you of your work. If you wish to remain a tantalizing question mark, I shall not reveal you."

"You are thinking I lack the courage of my convictions, to hold such strong views and not speak of them amongst my friends."

"I did not say so. I think you are wise, if you mean to live in Bath. In London, perhaps, the population are worldly enough to tolerate a little deviance from the norm, but in Bath, you would be ostracized."

"That is exactly why I do not speak of it," I said, grateful for his opinion. Actually I had less interest in the subject than he imagined. It was my gothic novel that occupied me at that time. "In any case, I am working on something else at this moment."

"Indeed?" He looked interested. Was he imagining me at work on some serious tome? "What is it?" he asked.

I blushed a little and said, "Poetry," for I once again lacked the courage to tell the truth.

"Ah."

"Nature poetry," I added feebly.

"I had heard it was unprofitable, except in a few rare cases such as Wordsworth. That is more usually a pastime the well-to-do indulge in. I hope you will permit me to read it before it is published. The *Quarterly* reviews a deal of poetry." He wore a curious look, wondering at this occupation when I had claimed in my essay to be a pauper.

I had no explanation, and was not inventive enough to come up with one on the spot. I was not unhappy with my little white lie, however. Wasting my time on a genteel hobby seemed to raise me in Paton's esteem. He mentioned that Lady Forrest was planning a rout in the near future, and said he would deliver a card to Lampards Street. Calling with a card from his aunt was a totally different matter than delivering me to examine a lovenest. Something had sparked his *proper* interest, and I was busy to fan the spark.

"Your aunt has asked me to call one day. I feel I am in an equivocal position, Lord Paton. Somehow the notion seems to have got afoot that you and I are—" I stopped and gave a helpless look.

"Yes, I, too, have felt the discomfort of it. I dare say it is Lady DeGrue's doing. She could not conceive of our being together at Corsham without the propriety of an understanding between us, or at least an inclination in that direction. It makes it difficult for us to become better acquainted."

"Just so. I have tried to explain, but once she takes an idea in her head, it is like talking to a table or a chair."

He smiled with something more than simple politeness. "Otherwise, I would have called on you sooner," he said.

I try to be sensible, and behave with at least a modicum of worldliness. It was annoying in the extreme to realize that this speech caused my heart to speed up. I willed down the emotion and replied blandly, "Perhaps the best thing is for us not to become better acquainted. I am sure you have any number of friends in town by now, and I, too, am beginning to know a few people."

"Now, there is a facer for me!" He laughed. "I was a mere stopgap, a filler-in until you met someone you liked better. Well enough to swell a scene or two, as the bard says, but no leading character in Miss Nesbitt's life."

"Indeed I did not mean anything of the sort. Now you are putting words in my mouth, sir!"

"That would be carrying coals to Newcastle. You have no deficiency of words."

I felt bereft of a clever reply all the same, and sat like a jug.

"Cat got your tongue, Miss Nesbitt? Or is it the subject that displeases you? Nothing has been settled about how we may meet each other without giving rise to the prospect of an imminent announcement. We could accidentally meet in the Pump Room one day. I had hoped we might do so before now, but I have not seen you there. With Isabel and Miss Potter for insulation, that might escape the quizzes' curiosity, don't you think?"

"Very likely. One meets the whole world in the afternoon at the Pump Room."

"Afternoon! That explains it. I have been hanging about in the morning."

"Early afternoon," I added nonchalantly. "I work in the morning, you see."

"Then I shall change my schedule, and also work in the morning. It is a better time for it actually. Business before pleasure."

"If you can call drinking that horrid water a pleasure."

"The horrid water is the price we must pay for the pleasure of meeting our—friends."

He hesitated a telling moment over the choice of word, which struck me as significant, so of course I had to pretend not to notice it. "Why do we continue this puritanical notion that any simple pleasure must be paid for by a matching hardship, I wonder?"

"Simple? I trust that does not refer to your friend's mental capacity! I am no genius, but I am not accustomed to hearing myself called simple. People are so kind. They say it only behind my back," he added with mock pensiveness.

With a memory of his former duplicity, I said rather sharply, "I doubt if anyone who knows you calls you anything of the sort, Lord Paton."

"Thank you—I think? Have you something to add to that peculiar judgment, Miss Nesbitt? There is a certain gleam in your eye that hints at an urge suppressed."

"Whatever can you mean?" I asked, and kept on gleaming at him, perhaps unwisely.

I watched him as he watched me. He would soon figure out that I knew what he had been about during that trip to Corsham if I was not careful. The question was there. He looked first confused, then wary. He would think me little better than a trollop if I agreed to go on seeing him, knowing his first intention, so I had to talk the suspicion away.

"I mean you are uncommonly sly, to hoodwink the quizzes, and further our acquaintance without putting your bachelorhood at risk."

He seemed to accept this awkward explanation. "A man's bachelorhood is always at risk when he is with a clever, pretty lady. That is a compliment, Miss Nesbitt. Pray feel free to blush or simper, or display any maidenly emotion you feel that poor effort merits."

I made a coquettish moue. "Oh, *pretty*, that merits nothing but a pout. If you *really* thought me pretty, you would have said beautiful."

"We shall not follow this line of reasoning, or you'll be accusing me of thinking you simple. Clever, I dare say, is French for stupid. I should have called you a genius. Unfortunately, I am in the habit of saying what I mean. It is an error we critics fall into if we are not careful."

"I was judging you in your other mode. That is the problem."

He cocked his head aside and looked at me from the corner of his eyes. "And what mode is that?"

"The mode of flirt, sir. They do not confine themselves to the awful truth."

He laughed. "Good Lord, have I learned to flirt, after all these years? If one persists, you see, he can learn anything, providing he has a good teacher."

I felt licensed to toss my shoulders and pout some more at this charge. We parted on excellent terms. Lord Paton came back for another lesson in flirting during dinner.

"Do you think this is wise?" I asked quietly with a smile to show I was not serious. "The quizzes will be taking the notion there really *is* something between us."

It was exactly the idea that was being reinforced between Ladies Forrest and DeGrue. I saw them exchanging knowing looks as Paton entertained me.

"We need expect no further punishment for the pleasure of our flirtation. This dinner is payment enough."

Dinner, which I forgot to mention, was a very inferior effort on Lady DeGrue's part. There was no lobster, no raised pies, but a few plates of cold meat and cheese which had been left uncovered for so long that they were all dry around the edges. The tea, needless to say, was as weak as water. I'm sure Lord Ronald despised the whole repast. He didn't eat a bite, and left immediately after. I noticed he had a private word with Isabel before leaving, and meant to learn what he said at the first opportunity.

Annie and I soon left as well. "I'll call on you tomorrow afternoon," Isabel said as we got our bonnets and pelisses. There were other ladies in the room, and we could not share any confidences.

"Let us go to the Pump Room," I suggested casually.

"No! To Crescent Gardens, at three-thirty."

My heart fell at this suggestion. Her naming a precise hour sounded like a pre-arrangement, and I felt in my bones it was Etherington's work. My concern for Isabel did not make me forget my appointment with Lord Paton at the Pump Room. I would have to talk her out of meeting Lord Ronald when she called tomorrow.

The drum was considered quite a success. Pepper was *aux anges* to get a toe into polite society, where he had been received better than he hoped. No one knew precisely what he published, and the simple act of publishing was no disadvantage. Annie was happy because he and I were happy. I felt I had firmed my position in society. Several ladies had invited me to call. It was becoming clear that I required a better address for I disliked to invite them to the top floor of Lampards Street. If only I were sure my gothic would sell, I would feel free to squander some of my savings in a move downtown, and the hiring of a servant.

With all the happenings of that night, the liveliest since coming to Bath, it was late when I went to bed, but I took a moment to jot a thought down in my diary. "My opinion of gentlemen has been both lowered and raised somewhat by tonight's doings with them. I met the sub-species, flirtus unscrupulus (lowered), and learned it is despised by proper gentlemen. More than one of them displayed very kind feelings toward the intended victim (raised). Gratified to discover this vestige of chivalry has survived."

Chapter Eleven

THE LITERARY MUSE, whom I envisaged as the ghost of Mrs. Radcliffe, sat on my shoulder all the next morning, whispering clever words into my ear. My composition was usually more inspired after a successful social outing. The time flew by and before I knew it, Isabel was tapping at the door. We were on close enough terms by then that I invited her into my bedchamber while I made my toilette for the outing.

She still wore traces of last night's exhilaration. It seemed a shame to bring her down from such ecstatic heights, but it had to be done. "Do hurry, Emma," she said, drawing out her watch and glancing at it.

Keeping all censure from my voice to tempt her into confession, I inquired, "Have you arranged to meet Lord Ronald this afternoon, Isabel?"

Her answer was a soft sigh. "Yes, at three-thirty."

"Why did you not ask him to call on you?"

"Oh, Auntie would not care for that! She feels he is not at all the thing."

"Then it is a great pity she invited him to her drum."

"She could hardly omit him when he was staying with his aunt, who is one of her bosom bows."

"I see." I set down my brush and turned a sapient eye on her. "And you truly expect me to help you slip around behind your aunt's back in this deception? That is a hard way to treat a friend, Isabel."

"But you said I should take control of my own life! I am the one with the money."

"Yes, and it is your money—nothing else—that interests Etherington. The whole world knows what he is, Isabel. How can you be such a gudgeon?"

She lifted her chin and pouted like a girl of five or six. Undeterred, I continued. "Perhaps I urged you too far toward freedom before you were ready for it. Choosing your own bonnets is quite different from choosing your own husband on such short acquaintance."

"But you said we ought not to be forced to marry anyone we dislike."

"No one is forcing you to marry anyone."

"Auntie is always pushing Sir Laurence Edwards at me" was the harshest treatment she could come up with. I had already begun to suspect that Lady DeGrue was not a complete ogre.

"Then you ought certainly to resist her if you cannot care for him, but Lord Ronald? What has *he* to recommend him, outside of a handsome face? He is a younger son who has fribbled away his fortune and run to Bath to escape the merchants. He has no idea of manners; he sulks; he despises everything— except a gullible heiress. Any gentleman who asks you to meet him in secret is up to no good, my girl. Please, for your own sake, don't meet him today."

Her chin descended an inch, but still rode higher

than usual. "He told me people would say that. I have a mind of my own. I know he is not perfect, but neither am I, Emma. And he says he will change once he is settled down. If I cannot buy some happiness with my money, what good is it to me?"

"You will not be buying happiness, but a few weeks' tumultuous excitement during the clandestine courtship, followed by a lifetime of remorse. Do you think he has any notion of making you happy? Think again!"

The chin remained high. Isabel, who used to be so shy and gentle, had become a perfect mule. "I have told him I shall meet him, and I shall. I am through with being trodden underfoot by Aun—anyone. If you do not care to accompany me, then I shall go alone." She looked from the corner of her eye to see if this threat moved me.

"I shall go, on one condition. That you do not see him in secret again. If he can indeed settle down, then let him show it by carrying on this courtship in the proper fashion." I mentally made another condition, viz., that we would rush, post haste, to the Pump Room as soon as we finished with Etherington.

"Very well," she said sullenly.

Our usual high spirits were considerably lowered as the carriage descended the downs to the Crescent Gardens. Annie accompanied us, but it was agreed she would not be told everything. In theory, we were to accidentally meet Etherington. I was to draw Annie aside and allow them a few moments privacy for Isabel to explain that she would not meet him by stealth again.

We got out of the carriage and began our stroll

through the gardens. I prayed that Etherington would not keep the assignation. That would give her an idea of his character. No such luck. He was there, lurking behind some bushes to leap out with unholy promptitude and glower in simulated surprise. He really was distressingly handsome. On this informal occasion, his cravat was replaced by a rakish dotted kerchief at his neck. His curls fell with seductive abandon over his pale brow, and his black eyes looked like obsidian. More rewriting! He was a perfect villain. I felt it would add something to my novel to make my villain physically attractive. Of course the eyes must carry a heavy burden to give a hint of the demon within.

"Miss Bonham!" he said with a degree of astonishment that would have pleased the audience of Drury Lane. "What a delightful surprise."

Isabel's acting lacked his dash. "Hello, Lord Ronald," she said guiltily. "You remember Miss Nesbitt, and Miss Potter."

"Ladies." His bow was somewhat casual, but not without grace. He came within an ace of smiling at me. He took me for either an accomplice or a tool in this romance.

Without further conversation he and Isabel began strolling in front of us, their heads together in earnest conversation. No matter how hard I strained my ears, I could hear very little. From the way he inclined his head to hers, I thought he was urging her on to further indiscretions. She appeared to be resisting.

Before we parted, I knew she had won the day. "I look forward to seeing you on Quiet Street tomorrow," he told her before he made his adieus and left, with a disillusioned shot at me from his dark eyes.

Isabel was now at peace with the world. She smiled demurely, casting a "so there" look upon me. I was relieved. I would make every effort to foil the villain, and if in spite of all he had his way, at least it would not be my fault. Lady DeGrue would prove a formidable opponent.

"Shall we go to the Pump Room?" was a logical suggestion, and found favor. I did not mention meeting Paton there, in case he failed me. But when we entered and took a table, he proved quite as prompt as Lord Ronald, and much more agreeable. He smiled, he sat down and ordered us a handsome tea with no nonsense about drinking the foul waters. He expressed his delight with Lady DeGrue's drum, and best of all when we had had one cup of tea, he suggested that he and I go for a walk and let Isabel and Annie enjoy the remainder of the pot.

This was how a suitor ought to conduct himself— with openness, consideration, and good humor. I hoped Isabel was making the comparison with Lord Ronald's behavior. The one contretemps of the afternoon was in no way Paton's fault. One could not expect Angelina, his former mistress, to move into a convent because they were through, but I felt it contrary of Fate to deliver her to that precise spot at that precise moment when our conversation was proving most agreeable. I did not know at the time who she was, but suspected, and had it confirmed later by Isabel.

Even under this trying circumstance, Paton proved a perfect gentleman. Angelina, clutching the arm of an aging but dapper roué, inclined her head and tossed a saucy smile at Paton. I noticed that her incredibly large and lustrous eyes soon skewed in my direction and raked me from head to toe. Paton nodded and smiled, no doubt giving her escort the same oracular examination as I had just endured. He did not stop, or mention her.

Unaware of her identity, I said, "What a lovely creature! Is she an actress?" There was that in her toilette that did not make the question a slight.

He tried to divert my thoughts with a joke. "As you call her lovely, I dare say you are thinking that her nose is crooked, or her jaw too long."

"Indeed I am not. She is exquisite."

Paton cast a flirtatious smile down on me and said, "She is well enough if a man has any taste for blond curls, flashing blue eyes, dimples, and an exceedingly well-filled gown."

"You prefer emaciated hags, I take it?"

"No, shrews—like you. Miss Newman, unfortunately, is not a great conversationalist."

I mentally stored up the name for future investigation. "One cannot have everything."

"If one qualification must be inferior, and I do not for a moment mean to imply that it is in the present company, I should prefer that it be appearance."

Thinking of Lord Ronald, I replied with strong feelings. "Beauty, and even brains, can be a positive curse if they are not matched with character."

He gave a conscious look. "I trust that you too mean to exclude present company. Or have you learned the truth about me, that my character is blackened beyond redemption?"

"Now, why should you think I am speaking of you? I said someone with beauty and brains."

"Revealed for the egotist I am! You spoke with

such passion, I thought you had one specific ne'er-do-well in mind. Ladies are not usually pitched into emotional violence by an abstract phenomenon."

I was tempted to mention Lord Ronald, but as that hurdle had been successfully passed, I did not. "Where did you get such a foolish idea? You think only men are concerned at injustice, and greed and knavery? I will have you know I wax very strong at all the social ills."

"Especially when the grocer puts his thumb on the scales, eh, Miss Nesbitt?"

"We are speaking of abstracts!" I said loftily. Then less loftily, "And it is my landlady I had in mind. She promised that fuel came with the rent, and now she tells me I must pay for the coal."

"If she suggests a particular coal merchant, don't use him. He'll up the price and give her a cut."

"I have half a mind to bust up the chairs and burn them. It would not be difficult. There isn't a leg in the lot that doesn't jiggle precariously when you sit on it."

Paton's face assumed a less frivolous tone. "I rather wondered that you chose such a—an inconvenient address."

"By which you mean a low address."

"Not at all. Lampards Street is quite an aerie. If you are thinking of removing, however, a friend of mine has a flat in the Westgate Buildings that he wishes to sublet. He's letting it go at a very good price, probably no more than you are paying now. Shall I speak to him?"

"That would be very kind of you, but—are you trying to make me respectable, Lord Paton?"

His smile can be described only as intimate. It

seemed to reach right out and touch me. "No, more easily accessible," he said.

"Any address is accessible to you. You have the stoutest pair of nags in all of Bath."

"They don't mind the ascent. It's trying to hold 'em in on the downgrade that is destroying all my gloves."

We had completed our circuit and returned to the table. "I could do with another cup of tea, but I expect it is all gone," I said.

"No problem. We'll pretend we're Lady DeGrue and order a gallon of hot water."

Of course he ordered a fresh pot, and the conversation became more general. I told Annie about the flat in the Westgate Buildings, and she talked it up for some time. After a proper interval, Lord Paton took his leave, saying that he would speak to Mr. Percival about the flat, and arrange with him a time for us to look it over.

"I'll go to speak to Percival right away. Then I shall whip up my nags, buy a new pair of gloves, and call on you this evening," he said. And with a bow, he was off, leaving nothing but good feelings behind.

"That is a stroke of luck for us." Annie smiled.

Again thinking of Etherington, I said, "It certainly shows great consideration on Paton's part. He is a real gentleman."

Isabel lifted a brow and said, "Yes, I noticed he was careful not to introduce you to Miss Newman, but passed as if he scarcely knew his mistress."

I jumped a foot. "Was that Angelina?"

"Yes, the pretty blonde with Mr. Hill," Isabel said. She lifted the pot and poured. I noticed she held it higher than before. Her confidence was soaring to dangerous heights, and it was all my fault.

We left soon after, and I stopped in to see Mrs. Speers before going up to our flat. It was too late to find her perfectly sober, but she was not yet bosky. Her hair had begun to tumble from its chignon, and the room smelled of juniper, but she was coherent.

"How is the biography going, Mrs. Speers?" I inquired. We all felt it a duty to inquire after Madame de Staël before proceeding to real business.

"I am just returning her to France, into the arms of Napoleon."

"Hands," I think, would have been a better choice of word. "How nice. I have come to let you know Miss Potter and I will very likely be leaving within a few days."

She shot a malevolent glare at me. "I'll need a week's warning, Miss Nisbett. Read your contract."

"Very well, consider this the warning. In fact, I shall put it in writing, as I failed to do regarding the coal."

"Now, dearie, if it's the coal, we can do something about that. I know a tradesman will give you a great bargain on it." I mentally translated this to read "give *me* a great bargain." "I *do* like to share my roof with ladies," she continued in her own ladylike way, "and there is no point pretending that Millie Pilgrim is anything but a trollop. Out till all hours again last night, but at least she didn't try to slip him into her room. As to Elinor Clancy, if her dad was a churchman, mine was a dook."

"It is not the coal, but the inaccessible location that distresses me," I assured her.

"I'll put Millie out and give you her rooms. It will save Miss Potter the last flight of stairs. Just give me a day or two to prepare her, or there will be feelings. Maybe Millie will take your third floor rooms," she added with a conniving look.

"I meant the address, Mrs. Speers. Lord Paton has found us a set of rooms in the Westgate Buildings."

She sniffed. "Lord Paton, is it? He never called on you but the once. If you think to trap that customer in a parson's mousetrap, think again, miss. It was a mistress-ship he had in mind, nothing else."

I bridled up like an angry mare. Customer indeed! "You betray your origins by such a speech as that, Mrs. Speers. You will have my letter of termination this evening, providing you are in any condition to read by that time."

She picked up her glass and took a long swig. "Pretty high and mighty for one of Pepper's hacks. I could buy and sell you. I received a check today for three hundred pounds, for novels that have been on the market a decade and are still being snatched up."

"Good for you!" I exclaimed, delighted to hear it.

She seemed confused by my response to her boast, which was obviously intended as a floorer. "Very kind of you to say so, I'm sure," she simpered, and returned me to the eminence of a lady. "We don't get your kind of class here often, Miss Nisbitt. I'll be sorry to see you go. Why don't you drop in and visit me sometime?"

"And you must visit me," I said rashly, wishing I had not told her our new address.

I went right upstairs and wrote my notice of termination. If Mr. Percival's rooms proved unsuitable for any reason, Mrs. Speers would be happy to hear it, and let us have our old rooms back. I pondered long over the affair of Lord Paton. He no longer suspected me of being a lightskirt, and still seemed interested in me. Barring that interest in the muslin company, he was very nearly the ideal parti.

But what would a duke's family think of Miss Nesbitt? They probably had some great and noble heiress in mind for him. It is not only ladies who are subject to coercive forces from society. He too would feel pressure to toe the matrimonial line. There was obviously no article for *The Ladies' Journal* in this line of thinking, and I put it aside for later consideration.

It was time to think of chops and potatoes, and making a fresh toilette before Paton called that evening.

Chapter Twelve

LORD PATON'S VISIT was brief. My hopes had soared to such unrealistic heights that I envisaged a visit of an hour or two, and had even prepared a platter of sliced ham and cheeses to magically present, to minimize the lack of a servant. I should have known when he showed up in formal evening attire that he was on his way to a party, but even that did not awaken me to reality. I thought he had gone to such extraordinary pains to impress me, and regretted my inferior brown sarsenet gown.

He sat down for a glass of wine at least, and gave us a pretty full description of Mr. Percival's rooms. They sounded superior in every way to those presently occupied, and at a rent low enough that Annie inquired about it.

"Mr. Percival signed a year's lease and must pay whether he occupies the space or not," Paton explained. "If the rooms are vacant for even a month, he will lose more than by subletting them immediately at a slightly lower rate. It is all mathematics, ladies. This gift horse comes with a full set of teeth."

"What hour did you set for us to see the rooms?" I asked.

"Three in the afternoon. I know you work in the morning, Miss Nesbitt. I thought we would go before visiting the Pump Room, if that suits you?"

"Excellent."

"So shall I pick you up at, say, two forty-five?"

"If you feel your gloves are up to it." I smiled, to show my appreciation without gushing.

"They are up to anything, like their wearer. And now I really must be off. I have literary colleagues visiting from London. I do not like to upset my aunt's regular card evening by landing them in on her. And after the dullness of Carleton House and Covent Garden and Hyde Park, they are eager to see some *real* sights. I thought dinner at the Pelican might impress them."

"Dr. Samuel Johnson." I nodded, as that is the inn's main claim to distinction.

"Spoken like a true Bath-ite. One dislikes to call the townsmen Bathers. It seems to suggest they are unique in their passion for water, and cast a slur on the bathing habits of the rest of the country."

"What *are* they called?" Annie asked. "Bathonians?"

"Quizzes, by and large," he replied. "And now that I have given Miss Nesbitt her daily insult, I shall take my leave before she retaliates. Tomorrow at two forty-five," he reminded us, and rose to gather up his hat and gloves.

I accompanied him to the door, said good evening, and he left. The sound of a man's footfall on the landing warned me that some other company was approaching, so I held the door open. Annie had not mentioned that Pepper was coming, but he kept in close enough touch that he usually knew when we would be in, and sometimes popped in unannounced.

I knew as soon as I saw the top of the man's head that it was not Pepper. The hat was too stylish. The gait too was faster than an elder man's would be. Who was it? I watched as the new arrival and Lord Paton exchange a glance in passing. Then the newcomer looked up and I recognized the face of Geoffrey Nesbitt.

My mind went blank. I could feel my face contort in a hideous parody of virtue outraged. I was aware, as if viewing the whole from a great height, that Paton turned and looked up at me. He hesitated a moment, uncertain whether he should leave me in such distress.

"Geoffrey!" I said in a strangled whisper.

Paton turned and began to remount the stairs again, casting suspicious looks at Geoffrey. "Emma, are you all right?" he called.

Geoffrey gave him a sharp look. "Who is this man, Emma?" he demanded.

My answer was to Paton, for I wanted above everything to get him out of the way before Geoffrey and I came to cuffs. "Yes, it's fine, Paton. Thank you. I can handle this."

He looked, waiting for an introduction. "Tomorrow," I called to him, and ushered Geoffrey into the flat.

The last I saw of Lord Paton was a worried frown, as he hovered, wondering what he should do. Then I turned to confront my cousin.

I have spoken in a derogatory way of Geoffrey, and would not want to leave you with the impression

142

that he is a physical monster. He is not at all ugly, just pompous. He is of medium height, with medium brown hair, fair to middling handsome. Mediocre in every way.

He put his hands on his hips like an outraged housekeeper and said, "This is a fine how-do-you-do, I must say, Emma. What do you mean by rushing away from Nesbitt Hall as though I were an ogre? Have you any idea of the sort of questions and insinuations I have been subjected to over the past weeks?"

"None, and I couldn't care less. You were well paid for any slight inconvenience my departure caused you."

His voice rose to dangerous heights. "Slight inconvenience! That is putting it mildly. The neighbors half believe I have done away with you."

"Nonsense. Annie corresponds with half a dozen of them. They know perfectly well how the situation stands, that she and I are living in this hovel because my father gave you all our money."

He began pacing the floor. "Well, if that isn't just like a woman! To go dashing off, imagining herself a put-upon heroine."

"Dramatics aside, you cannot believe I am *not* put upon!"

"You have brought any hardship endured upon yourself."

"I prefer my present circumstance to being your wife," I snapped. "It seems that is the only alternative my father left. Everything—house, money, consuls—all were given to you, carte blanche."

"I had nothing to say about that. I was astonished when I heard the will read."

"You were in seventh heaven!" I charged. "Do you think I'm blind? I saw you smirking into your collar, trying not to shriek for joy as the will was read. It was your giving my father those damned French books to read that did the mischief in the first place, and don't pretend you were unaware of Mr. Rousseau's philosophy, for I am not an idiot."

"Now, Emma," Annie said placatingly.

"Don't either of you try 'now-Emma-ing' me. It was infamous." Hot tears scalded my eyes at the memory of that dreadful morning. I blinked them away and continued with my tirade, for if I did not, I felt I would burst. Geoffrey Nesbitt was the very incarnation of my doom.

Geoffrey twitched at his collar and tried not to gloat. "It is true I feared you would play ducks and drakes with your father's fortune," he admitted. "The estate was entailed upon me, there was no injustice in *that*. I *did* think your father would leave you the bulk of the money. . . ."

"And were at pains to forestall him!"

"Your father—and I—wanted you to continue living where you were born and raised. A marriage between us was the logical, reasonable thing. I dare say your father thought you likelier to comply if you—"

"If I had no say in the matter!" I flung back angrily. "If the alternative was poverty. That is a fine, Christian point of view. I wonder he did not hire a pen of lions to ensure my accepting. And let me tell you, Geoffrey, I would *rather be* eaten alive by lions than marry you!"

He stiffened up. "I have come to make an alternative arrangement, one that does not include a *pride* of lions," he said, emphasizing the word "pride." It is exactly the sort of pedantry that infuriates me with Geoffrey. He will think of semantics, or whatever it is called, at such a critical moment as this. "It was never your father's—or my—intention to see you penniless. Naturally we discussed the eventuality that you refused to have me. Your father trusted me to behave in a gentlemanly manner if that happened. If you are convinced we do not suit—"

I snorted like a penned bull. He glared, and continued. "If you wish to set up a separate residence, naturally some equitable settlement must be made. It was what your father wanted."

This fell on my ears like celestial music. I stopped ranting and stared in disbelief. "What do you mean?"

"I have discussed it with my solicitors. Your father left approximately fifty thousand pounds in cash and investments. Some of it will be required to run the Hall."

"It more than pays for itself!"

"Very true, but the whole of the sum was left to me. Your father and I decided, and my solicitor thinks it a generous settlement, on splitting the fifty thousand equally."

Though I am no mathematician, it did not take me long to latch on to the sum of twenty-five thousand pounds. I was delighted, but with my recent practice in haggling with Mrs. Speers. I tried to up the sum. "Which leaves you, a mere cousin, with an estate worth fifty thousand easily, and twenty-five thousand cash."

"The mother's dowry is usually given to the daughter. Your mother's dot was twenty-five. That is the sum your father determined," he said stiffly. "I have the papers here," he added, and patted his pocket.

The cliché about the bird in the hand popped into my head. Geoffrey was not obliged by law to give me so much as the steam off his porridge. I gracefully relented and said, "Well, if Papa thought twenty-five thousand was fair . . ."

"Generous! That is very generous, Geoffrey," Annie exclaimed. "Why, Emma, we can look higher than a set of sublet rooms in the Westgate Buildings. We can hire a house."

All was restored to peace, and even jollity. We had wine, and later the platter of ham and cheese prepared for Paton. Annie and I made light of the travails of managing without a servant.

"It is infamous to see you living like this!" Geoffrey exclaimed, but not in his usual toplofty fashion. He was so happy to be free of having to marry me that he was nearly giddy. He had no more love for me than I for him, but is one of those gentlemen who will do anything for money. "We must see you removed to a decent place, and servants hired before I leave. Then I can return to Milverton with my head held up."

"I shall have twelve hundred and fifty pounds per annum. We are rich, Annie!" I laughed.

"Lord Paton will be surprised to hear of your change in fortune." This had occurred to me long since, but it did not seem the time to mention it.

"Is that the fellow who was scowling at me on the stairs as I came up?" Geoffrey inquired.

"Yes." I blushed.

"Surely he is not the Duke of Crannock's son and heir!"

"Yes," I said again.

"Good God! Don't tell me you have nabbed a *marquess*. My generosity was not necessary."

This pernicious idea had to be talked away at once. "Good gracious, he is only a friend. I have not nabbed him."

"But you might, with twenty-five thousand pounds," Annie said.

"That would be an excellent connection." Geoffrey beamed. Titles rank second only to hard cash in his hierarchy of virtues. I think he would gladly part with my dowry to be able to claim such a connection. "How did you meet him? I thought he lived in London. And of course his family seat is in Kent."

"He is visiting an aunt in Bath," I explained.

"And since you are in mourning, he cannot take you out to assemblies or such things," Geoffrey said. He noticed my toilette. "I say, Emma, a brown gown is a little unusual, is it not? What must Lord Paton have thought?"

Annie answered for me. "Oh, we were staying in, you know, so it did not seem to matter. Paton is not fastidious."

"Just so you observe all the proprieties when you go out with him."

A whole swamp of difficulties rose up in my mind's eye. I hadn't brought a stitch of mourning with me. How was Geoffrey to take us about, hiring a house and servants, without soon being privy to the fact?

He must be got rid of as soon as possible, and till that time, I must develop some indisposition that put me securely in bed. I soon began coughing delicately into my fist, and said my throat felt a little rough. I inquired where he was staying so that I might send him a note in the morning putting off our house-hunting. I did not mean to be so ill that the solicitor could not come to settle the payment, however. He soon left, and Annie and I settled down to scheming.

She was fully alive to the necessity of my becoming ill. "We'll ask Geoffrey to bring the solicitor here. We must send Paton a note as well, and explain that we will not be requiring Mr. Percival's rooms," she added.

"Yes, certainly, but do not give the reason yet, Annie. I will tell him in my own way, and in my own time."

"I'll write, and explain that you are feeling poorly."

"Yes, but tell him we will not be taking the rooms, for Percival will want to find someone else. I must write to Isabel too. I am so relieved that we straightened out the business of Lord Ronald before this came up. Lady DeGrue will be on the alert to protect her now."

"Will you continue writing for Arthur?" Annie asked later.

"No, I shall concentrate on my novel. Mrs. Speers is making a fortune. Besides, it's fun. But I shall find it difficult to keep in the gloomy groove with all this good fortune. Isn't it lovely being rich again, Annie? We'll visit London one of these days."

Anything that removed her from Bath and Arthur received short shrift. "I don't see how London cannot be much nicer than Bath," she said.

It was not a night for retiring early. Annie wrote all the necessary notes to give the pretence that I was ill, then we sat talking over wine. Annie would lend me a mourning gown for the solicitor's visit, to fool Geoffrey. After we had ironed out these little difficulties, we planned out our future and mentally spent our fortune a dozen times. Eventually we did go to bed.

For the first time since the reading of the infamous will, I was at peace with my father. I even shed a private tear in memory. He had not meant to disinherit me, nor was Geoffrey such a deep-dyed villain as I feared. In my diary I acknowledged that two more sub-species of gentleman had earned redemption in my eyes. Fathers and cousin-suitors were allowed to possess a degree of fairmindedness. At this rate there would be nothing left but Frenchmen to disparage. I dare say all Frenchies did not admire Rousseau, if it came to that.

It had been precipitous of me to dash away from home without having even *tried* to reach a settlement with my cousin. And that essay! I was in a mood to assume mourning for Papa now, and soon realized that it was impossible to do so in Bath. Unless I claimed I had just learned of my father's death . . . No, that would not do. I had already implied to friends that he had been dead for a year. Oh, what a tangled web we weave . . .

But it would work out somehow. It is impossible to be depressed when you have a set of papers turning twenty-five thousand pounds over to you. And a marquess lurking in the shadows. Even a duke would not turn up his nose at twenty-five thousand pounds. If Geoffrey could give me a handle to my name, it would be even better, but titles were not his to give, or he would have one himself. He would probably marry some noble lady now. My last totally unworthy thought was that even if he did, he would still be only Mr. Nesbitt, while I would be the Marchioness of Paton. I would precede him in to dinner, if Paton and I ever visited Nesbitt Hall.

Chapter Thirteen

IT IS CERTAINLY not my intention to blame it all on Annie, but I *do* wish I had written those notes of explanation myself. I would have made them less ambiguous. It was bad enough that Isabel came to call the next afternoon, when Annie was supposed to have made clear I was too ill to receive visitors. Isabel very nearly caught me up and about, looking a fright in one of Annie's black gowns. I managed to scuttle into my bedchamber and get a blanket up under my chin before she saw me. This, of course, made it impossible for me to remove so much as an arm from under the coverings. The mad scurry made my face red, and she thought I was much iller than I was. What I mean is, she thought I was truly ill, and kept her distance. I did not encourage her to come nearer the bed, nor to linger.

Even in my agitated condition, I could see she was upset. We called a few words across the room, and before she left I asked, "How did Lord Ronald's visit go, Isabel?" That, surely, was the cause of her condition.

An unshed tear shone in her eye, and when she replied, her voice was unsteady. "Auntie was dreadfully rude," she said, tossing her curls. "She did not even offer him a glass of wine, and when I did, she said he was in too much of a hurry to stay. Naturally he left very soon after that, for Ronald is very sensitive to a slight. And now you've gone and taken a cold. How can I see him? How can I explain?"

"No explanation is necessary, Isabel. I trust he understands the situation. His advances are not welcome. If he is a gentleman, he will cease pestering you. And if he is not, you will want nothing to do with him in any case."

She gave me a mutinous glare. "But they *are* welcome! I thought *you* would understand. Ronald is very intelligent and sensitive and handsome. Don't you think he is handsome, Emma? Everyone says he looks like Lord Byron. He can handle the ribbons like a top fiddler, and quote Latin and Greek."

There was a deal more of the same. She gave me to understand Lord Ronald was good at everything in the world except making an honest living, and I kept reiterating that he was a fortune hunter.

In the end, Isabel gave up in disgust and said, "If you were not ill, you would be in a better mood, and more helpful. Let me know as soon as you are able to go out again, Emma. I must go now."

She whisked out of the room, eyes flashing, and ran right into Geoffrey and the solicitor, just entering the flat. I waited on nettles to hear how Annie mishandled this contretemps. But when Geoffrey espies a pretty heiress, he seldom permits anyone else to hold the floor. Annie introduced them to each other, and from then on the voice heard through the door was Geoffrey's, with an occasional mumble from Isabel, who was in a hurry to leave. I hoped she would not do something foolish about meeting Lord Ronald.

As soon as Isabel said good-bye, I leapt out of bed, put on my slippers, and tidied my hair. The signing of the papers took only minutes. We required two witnesses. Annie was one; for the other, we called in Mr. Bellows, the least shameful of our fellow tenants. The solicitor had deposited my twenty-five thousand pounds in a bank in Bath, and handed me the book. I had only to go the bank and give them a specimen of my signature, and I could go on my spending spree.

We served wine to celebrate this joyful occasion. Bellows's eyes were goggling out of their sockets. When the solicitor rose to leave, I put a hand on Bellows's arm and accompanied him to the door as well. "What has happened, Miss Nesbitt?" he inquired. "As you are in mourning, I assume someone close to you has died. How fortunate you are to have wealthy relatives." He had managed to get a glimpse at what he was signing.

Not thinking, and wishing only to be rid of him, I said, "It is merely a transfer of funds to my name to permit me to live independently."

"But why are you wearing Miss Potter's black gown? Is it your cousin who has—" He looked askance at Geoffrey, trying to discern whether a match was hatching, or if he might try his hand with me again.

"I would prefer if this could remain our little secret," I said coyly. "You will not tell the others."

"Certainly not!"

He left, but I had a sinking feeling he would be back, soon and often. The next move was to get rid of Geoffrey. "Well, Emma," he said as he smiled, "shall we go down to the bank and finish up the papers, or are you eager to begin looking for a house? I have been going through the advertisements in the paper . . ."

"Did Annie not explain that I am not feeling well?" I inquired. I dare say I looked a perfect picture of health. Joy and excitement will brighten the eyes and lend a healthy hue to the cheeks. "I crawled from my bed only to sign the papers. I mean to return there immediately."

"Tomorrow, then."

"I'm sure you are very busy at the Hall, Geoffrey. Pray do not feel obliged to linger on my account. Annie and I can handle the bank work."

"But you will want a carriage to go looking for houses."

"I shall buy one."

He laughed as if I had suggested buying a warship. "A pair of green ladies will not want to undertake that without a man to help them."

"We know a few gentlemen. One of them will be happy to assist us."

"Lord Paton!" he exclaimed. "Yes, by Jove, that is an excellent excuse—*reason,* to call on him. Where does he live, Emma?"

"I would really prefer if you do not call on Lord Paton. Actually it is Annie's friend who will assist us. Mr. Pepper is an excellent judge of horseflesh."

"Pepper? Pepper?" He frowned. "I never heard you speak of a Mr. Pepper, Annie. What relation is he to you?"

"A very good friend—from Ireland," she said vaguely.

"You ladies have certainly scraped up a large circle of friends in a short time. That Miss Bonham seemed a well-bred sort of girl. Very pretty too. Would she be some kin to the Bonhams from Surrey?" Geoffrey inquired.

"She lives with her aunt, Lady DeGrue," I said, also vaguely.

"Bound to be the same family. Bonham is not at all a common name. Norman blood, I should think. At least it has a Frenchified sound to it. If that's who she is, she is related to half the nobility of Britain."

"And a fortune besides," Annie unwisely added.

"A pity we could not have gone out with her," Geoffrey said.

"Yes," Annie said, nodding, "for she will be gypped of her visit to the Pump Room. She will not want to go alone, but perhaps she will go home and ask her aunt to accompany her."

I, in my innocence, felt nothing but joy when Geoffrey rose to leave. "I shall return tomorrow and see how you go on," he said. "Meanwhile, I'll begin looking about for a carriage and team."

"Please, don't bother. You will be missed at home, Geoffrey. You really ought to get back to the Hall," I urged.

"I can spare a week to visit my cousin," he insisted, and left at once.

A week! As soon as the door closed, Annie turned a knowing face in my direction. "He's on his way to the Pump Room to dangle after Isabel," she said.

"She won't be there. She'll be at the Crescent Gardens. Better Geoffrey than Lord Ronald, in any case.

Lady DeGrue gave Etherington short shrift. I hope Isabel doesn't do something foolish."

It was soon revealed that Mr. Bellows had been broadcasting my good fortune through the house. Mrs. Speers came pounding upstairs. She had just finished work. Her thumb and index finger were black with ink, and her hair was like a haystack, but at least she was sober. "Is it true?" she demanded. "You have come into a fortune, Miss Nisbitt? I wondered when you told me you were leaving yesterday. I told Mr. Bellows it could not be as much as twenty-five thousand, or you would take a house, not rooms in the Westgate Buildings. Twenty-five hundred, was it?"

"I told Mr. Bellows not to say anything!"

She gave me a very sly look. "What is the secret, Miss Nisbitt? A scandal never rests unknown for long in Bath. If you have taken a cher ami, the ton will know all about it in a matter of days—hours. Is it Paton?" she inquired greedily.

"No! How dare you suggest such a thing!"

I did not want her retailing this slanderous idea, and to ingratiate her, I poured a glass of wine while deciding what to tell her. She would have preferred gin, but was no foe to alcohol in any form.

"The money was left to me by a relation," I said. "Lord Paton has nothing to do with it. The man Mr. Bellows met was a Mr. Nesbitt. I am surprised he did not tell you so."

"He said he called himself Nisbitt, but then, he would, wouldn't he, if he was trying to put a decent face on the matter?"

"The matter *is* decent! I have inherited some money. Surely that is nothing new in life."

She finished her glass and poured herself another.

The second glass made her mellow. "It sounds like a novel," she said dreamily. "Only I shall have Emmeline truly believe the money comes from an uncle, only to discover after she has spent most of it on charity—orphans perhaps—that it comes from the villain, who now has her in thrall."

Annie hid the bottle, and I assisted Mrs. Speers downstairs in case she should trip and kill herself. "How wretchedly everything is turning out!" I said when I returned. "I had not thought getting hold of a fortune would be so terribly unpleasant."

"It wouldn't be if you hadn't come here under false pretences." Annie sulked. The enervating events of the day were grinding at her nerves too.

Wine had worked to soothe the savage Mrs. Speers, and Annie and I decided to give it a try. It helped a little, but the good of the first glass was undone by the arrival of a note from Lord Paton. When I read it, I deeply regretted having left the writing of the notes to Annie.

Dear Miss Nesbitt,

I am sorry to hear you are not feeling well. I am not quite clear regarding Miss Potter's instructions. Do you wish me to put off Mr. Percival re the rooms till you are feeling better, or to inform him you are not interested at all? And if not, why not, if you don't mind a friend's vulgar curiosity? You won't find a better bargain elsewhere. I look forward to hearing from you. Hope you are feeling better tomorrow.

Regards, Paton

"Annie, I told you to tell Paton we did not want the rooms! What did you say?"

"That is exactly what I did tell him. I told him you were ill, and we did not want the rooms. I don't see how we could have misunderstood."

There was nothing wrong with Paton's understanding. In her excitement, Annie had said some such thing as I was ill, and could not see the rooms. I wrote an answer myself, and made it perfectly clear that we did not want the rooms, but were thankful for his efforts on our behalf. Ingenuity failed me in the matter of an excuse for the death of our interest, and I said only that his vulgar curiosity would be satisfied when next we met. This would not occur until Cousin Geoffrey was bounced back to Milverton, if I had anything to say about it. Having painted him an ogre in my essay, I did not want Paton to meet such an obliging person. Geoffrey, Papa, and the will were the only excuses I had to offer for my unconventional behavior.

We took what pleasure we could from reading the papers left by the solicitor and envisaging a future free of money woes. The money brought so many difficulties with it that I half thought I should return to Milverton with Geoffrey, or perhaps go to London. Receiving a fortune from the death of a relative definitely required mourning. Strict mourning definitely precluded enjoying my wealth. I foresaw a troubled future of explaining my situation to such sly and curious questioners as Lady DeGrue. She would not be put off with half answers. And then was Mrs. Speers, as well as accusing me of being a lightskirt.

We discussed it till dinnertime, then had dinner and discussed it some more. "Everything looks blacker at night," Annie consoled me. She was dead set against returning to Milverton for a period of mourning. She was so captivated by Pepper that she did not wish to leave him. And to tell the whole truth, I was not at all eager to leave Paton. "We'll think about it tomorrow," she told me.

The next day brought new troubles. I scampered into the bedroom when the door knocker sounded, and through the panel I heard a mumble of voices. The first distinguishable one was Geoffrey's, asking how I was.

"She's coming along," Annie assured him.

To my horror, I heard Isabel's higher voice asking, "May I go in to see her, Miss Potter?"

"I'll just see if she's awake," Annie replied, and came to my door. We held our brief conversation in whispers.

"Did they arrive together?" I demanded.

"Yes, he found out at the Pelican where she lives, and went to call yesterday. Such encroaching manners. He laid the butter on with a trowel, and Lady DeGrue allowed Isabel to drive out with him today."

"Good God, then DeGrue and Isabel know the truth about me."

"I don't know what he told them."

"You had best send him in."

"Isabel wants to see you. He didn't ask to."

"Send him in first. Tell him something urgent has arisen."

Annie ducked out, and in a moment Geoffrey's glowering visage was at the door. "Emma, I am shocked at you!" he said accusingly. "Imagine my horror to learn you have been jauntering about to balls and parties as though your father were not still warm in his grave."

"You didn't tell them!"

"Of course not," he snapped. "Your behavior reflects on me. I gaped when Lady DeGrue told me she met you at an assembly at the Upper Rooms. She was delighted that Miss Bonham has acquired such a lively yet perfectly respectable friend. I tried to cover my gaping by saying you were not usually much interested in social doings, but she looked suspicious. And how are we to account for your sudden wealth if we don't tell them your father just died?"

I made sure Geoffrey would have revealed me for the farouche creature I am, and suspected the fact that Lord Paton had befriended me had something to do with his reticence.

"I can hardly tell them that!" I snapped back.

"I have been conjuring with this knot all day, and have a suggestion. We could leave for Milverton immediately, say your father is ill, and not announce for a few days that he is dead. Then you can return to Bath—in mourning—and resume your friendships."

"That's impossible. I've already told them he died a year ago."

Geoffrey pondered this a moment. "We could say an uncle died, or an aunt. Lady DeGrue inquired about the black mourning band I am wearing. Fortunately she asked *after* I had learned of your active social life. I said that a cousin had died, which is true, as far as it goes."

"Then this cousin could have left me his worldly goods, you mean?"

"Precisely, and you will go into mourning at once."

"But I don't want to go into mourning, Geoffrey."

"Have you no proper feelings, no gratitude, no shame, no sense of responsibility to your family?"

"Of course I have—some. You know Papa and I were never close. Anger buried all proper feelings at first, but now that things are straightened out, I feel perfectly wretched. I am very sorry Papa is dead, but decking myself out like a carrion crow for a year will not bring him back. And saying a cousin died will only complicate matters later if anyone learns the real truth. Bath is a cauldron of gossip, Geoffrey. You have no idea."

What I did not say was that the one of main interest to me already knew the truth, and did not cut me because of it. The idea was taking root that I should tell all. It would be a nine day's wonder, the disinherited daughter who scorned society's rules and did not don black crape. If Paton stood beside me, and providing I became a pattern card of grief upon receipt of what was rightfully due me, I might be forgiven. Noble friends and a fortune will go a long way in that respect. But it left me with the onerous duty of mourning at that period of my life when I wanted more than ever before to get on with my life. Still, I felt it must be done, and suggested this course to Geoffrey.

He looked like a wild man. "You mustn't think of it!" he exclaimed. "You'll be ruined. Lady DeGrue will cut you dead. She won't want anything to do with anyone connected to you. And I might as well say, Emma, that I am very fond of Isabel. It is my intention to remain in Bath till I win her hand."

It was useless. The proper course might be best for me in the long run, but I did not want to harm

Geoffrey's chances. A new suitor might be the very thing to turn Isabel's thoughts from Etherington. "Then what is to be done?" I asked.

"Nothing, for the moment. You are not able to go out."

"I am *dying* to go out! I only pretended to be ill because I didn't bring any mourning clothes, and didn't want you to know."

"Such cunning! Such treachery! I thought I knew you, Emma. You are not at all what I took you for. A lady like Miss Bonham would never—"

"Would she not? Don't delude yourself that she is anyone's pawn, or that she cares for you. She is hot after a noble fortune hunter who is hot after her money. She will come to worse grief than I if I don't stop her."

Geoffrey turned pale. "Not Lord Ronald?"

"Yes, how did you know?"

"Everyone knows Lord Ronald. He is a byword for his profligacy. She wanted to alight from my carriage in the Crescent Gardens and speak to him. I, like a fool, allowed her to have a word with him in private."

"It would not surprise me in the least if they are laying plans for more clandestine meetings. Her aunt snubbed Lord Ronald, you must know. He will not dare return to the house."

He raked his hand through his hair. "Here is a pretty kettle of fish. Should I warn Lady DeGrue?"

"Certainly."

"But if she hears of it, Miss Bonham will despise me. She already thinks me a pretty stuffy sort of fellow."

"If you *don't* do it, she will bolt to Gretna Green and get herself shackled to Etherington."

Geoffrey looked momentarily beaten. "He is so very handsome too, to say nothing of having a title, even if he is only a younger son."

"I don't believe the title has much appeal for Isabel," I said. "She never speaks of such things."

"Of course," he said admiringly. "She *is* one of the Surrey Bonhams. Lady DeGrue confirmed it. Half her family have handles to their names. That would be nothing new to her."

Our tête-à-tête was interrupted by a tap on the door, and Isabel peeped her head in. "May I join you?" she asked, and came tripping up to the bed. "Oh, you're dressed, Emma! I thought you were in bed."

"Just malingering. A headache," I explained, and held my hand to my forehead to substantiate this lie.

"I shan't stay a moment. Why are you wearing that horrid old dark gown?"

Geoffrey gave me a quelling look and spoke before I could. "Emma has just learned of our cousin's death. You remember your aunt mentioned it yesterday. As she has no mourning gowns with her, she borrowed one from Miss Potter."

"I'm sorry to hear it," Isabel said. She did not inquire as to the exact degree of kindred existing between the victim and myself, nor did we encourage such talk. She turned to Geoffrey and said, "We ought not to pester Emma when she has the megrim, Mr. Nesbitt. Let us continue our drive."

"Stay for a moment, Isabel," I said. "We would like a moment alone, Geoffrey. Girl talk, you understand."

He left, and Isabel cast a sheepish eye on me. "You have seen Lord Ronald," I charged.

She pouted. "I just wanted to apologize for Auntie's rudeness."

"Please don't see him again, Isabel. There are better men than Etherington for the taking."

She twitched her shoulders and pouted. "No one ever bothers with me."

"How can you say so? Cousin Geoffrey has been singing your praises this quarter hour."

She looked pleased at this. "What did he say?"

"I shan't tell you, or your bonnet won't fit."

"Does he think I'm pretty?"

"Vastly pretty."

"Ronald says I have eyes the shade of cornflowers."

I made little of this. "What a hackneyed piece of flattery! He cannot even bother to compliment you as you deserve. If this is a sample of his poetry, it is as bankrupt as he is. Geoffrey thought your eyes were like star sapphires, and your skin like rose petals."

Her lips curved in delight. I had not thought Isabel to be a vain creature, but she was thrilled to death. "You're making that up!"

"Indeed I am not."

She tossed a saucy look over her shoulder. "If he were not such a dull old stick, I might take him for a flirt."

"Geoffrey, dull!" I laughed in well-simulated disbelief. If the silly chit wanted romance and danger and intrigue, let her have it from a harmless source. "They would be astonished to hear you say so where I come from. He acts the dullard to disarm the unwary. You must not tell your aunt he is such a rakish fellow, or she won't permit you to drive out with him again. He has not been too fast, I hope?"

She wore an expression between offense and interest. "Not at all."

"I have warned him to behave," I said. "You must not breathe a word of the duel."

Her eyes grew an inch. "Mr. Nesbitt fought a duel! Oh! I wonder if Ronald ever has."

"I shouldn't think so. He despises physical violence, does he not? I seem to recall he thought the pen mightier than the sword," I invented slyly.

She was eager to rejoin Geoffrey after that. They took their leave before I could inform him of his new persona as a dangerous, sword-wielding rake.

"You will call this evening, Geoffrey?" I asked rather imperatively. He read the language of the eye and knew something was afoot.

Chapter Fourteen

THAT EVENING GEOFFREY returned to learn what message I had for him, and was outraged that I had blackened his character.

"A duel!" he howled. "Good God, if Lady DeGrue ever hears such a story, my hopes are doomed."

"You *have* no hopes, unless Isabel mistakes you for something other than a dullard."

He accepted this description with a self-righteous, hurt look. "Between the two of us, we have told more lies today than I ever told in my life before," he grouched.

Yet he did not look so very sad. There was an air of febrile excitement about him. "Did you tell Lady De-Grue about Isabel's meeting Lord Ronald?" I asked.

"I did, and felt like a cad to do it. She was very appreciative, however. She wants me to entertain Miss Bonham till you are recovered, Emma. I am taking her on a drive to Claverton Down tomorrow. Perhaps Lady DeGrue will accompany us. She is to let me know this evening."

"You are returning this evening?" Annie asked.

"By invitation. Lady DeGrue had planned to take Miss Bonham to the Lower Rooms, but as I am in mourning, we could not go there," he explained. "She fears Miss Bonham had laid plans to meet Lord Ronald. The scoundrel will be out in his reckoning if that was what he had in mind."

Geoffrey looked more emotional than I had ever seen him look before. His nostrils flared, and the muscles in his jaws jerked a little. I sensed he was becoming truly fond of Isabel, and thought the better of him for it.

"Then we shan't detain you, Geoffrey," I said. "Give my regards to Lady DeGrue and Isabel. And remember, you are a wicked flirt. Be sure to tell Isabel she is beautiful, with eyes like star sapphires and skin like rose petals."

"Good God, she would laugh in my face. You have been reading those trashy novels again, Cousin."

"Perhaps you should try one, to learn what would please a lady. Say something outrageous when you get Isabel alone."

He walked differently when he left the flat. There was a bounce in his step. His hat sat at a jauntier angle. His smile held a hint of daring.

It was this dashing gent that Lord Paton would have seen leaving the building when he arrived. He came up the stairs not two minutes after Geoffrey left. I had the strange feeling that the souls of the two men had changed bodies as they passed. Dashing, daring Lord Paton came in wearing a frown that belonged on my cousin. His tread was measured, though not at all slow.

"Miss Nesbitt," he said through thin lips. He performed a jerky bow and added, "Miss Potter."

"Lord Paton, what a surprise!" I exclaimed. My first response was delight, which soon blended with discomfort as I recalled I was ill.

"I am relieved to find you well enough to receive callers," he said stiffly.

"Oh, you mean Geoffrey? That was my cousin."

"He is certainly solicitous. He also called the other evening, if I am not mistaken. You were less happy to see him then, to judge by your expression."

I rapidly canvased my mind for an excuse, and said, "We had a falling out when last we met. We have mended the breach, and are on terms again. Do sit down. Will you have a glass of wine?"

His eyes fell on the table, already littered with used glasses. Annie darted them to the kitchen to wash, as we only had four crystal ones. He sat, but not in the relaxed pose of a caller settling in for a chat.

"I came to have my vulgar curiosity satisfied, as you suggested in your note, Miss Nesbitt. Has your deciding against Percival's flat something to do with Mr. Nesbitt's return to favor?"

"Oh, no! That is, yes, in a way, I mean . . ." I felt the blood rush up my neck, and stammered like an apprehended thief.

His brown eyes burned into me. "What is it, yes or no? Has your cousin convinced you to leave Bath?"

"Our plans are not settled yet, but in fairness to Mr. Percival, I did not wish to keep his flat off the market."

"But you are contemplating leaving? You must be. The other flat is preferable in every way to this one."

"Actually, me might hire a house."

"A house! Your cousin sounds extremely generous." This was accompanied by a stare of maximum curiosity bordering on the impertinent. It demanded an explanation, which I was in no mood to give.

"I would hardly say that," I said, and dropped the subject like a live coal. "How did the meeting with your literary friends go, Lord Paton?"

"Fine. You have made a remarkably speedy recovery, Miss Nesbitt. I had not thought to have the pleasure of actually seeing you this evening. I hoped for no more than a word with Miss Potter."

"I am feeling very much better, thank you."

"I wonder your cousin didn't accompany you to the Lower Rooms for the assembly, as you are so wonderfully cured of whatever ailed you," he said in an ironical tone.

"Oh, Geoffrey is in mourning," I blurted out, and blushed again.

Paton's eyes narrowed. "So I gathered by the lavish display of crape. Is it for anyone we know?" he asked in a peculiarly insinuating voice.

My guilty answer came out in a muffled whisper. "Yes." I would reveal all to Paton, and try to enlist his support.

To my utter astonishment, he leapt from his chair and lunged in my direction. Before I knew what was happening, he was at my feet, grabbing me by both hands. It was in this melodramatic pose that Annie saw us when she arrived with the wine. She took one open-mouthed look and disappeared. I knew perfectly well she thought she was interrupting a proposal, and wished she had stayed.

"Emma, tell me the truth," Paton said in impassioned accents. "Is that man the bounder who stole your fortune in an effort to make you have him?"

"Geoffrey is my father's heir, but really the situation is of my own making."

He was suddenly on the sofa beside me. First he lifted my hands to his lips and kissed them warmly. I cannot imagine how I must have looked, but I felt shocked and thrilled to death. Paton put an arm protectively around my shoulders and pulled me against his chest, murmuring in my ear, "It's not your fault, Emma darling. I know none of this is your fault."

"It is really not Geoffrey's either—"

He straightened himself up and said more loudly, "Don't try to protect him! I'll call him out, the bastard! How dare he come here, trying to coerce you into marrying him."

"No, Paton. You misunderstand. It is not marriage he has in mind."

His eyes flew open. "Good God! He didn't try to *force* himself on you!"

I opened my lips to object, and was suddenly wrapped in a crushing embrace that took the breath out of me. Paton's lips moved in a frenzy of nibbling kisses over my ears and eyes and lips. "Poor Emma! And here I have been thinking ill of you. I should be beaten. I should have remained that first night. I was half afraid he'd try something, but you told me you could handle him. And Miss Potter was here. That will teach me to hold back my feelings. Emma—" He gazed at me from darkly glazed eyes.

I was speechless at this unexpected outpouring. I felt hot tears gathering in my eyes. It was all so strange and surprising and lovely to be loved. I felt a smile tremble on my lips. Before I said anything, Paton lowered his head and firmed my quivering lips with his. It was like a spark to tinder. A flame leapt between us, and for a long moment we were locked in a burning, passionate kiss that slowly subsided to mere ecstasy.

Paton looked a little embarrassed when he realized how he had gotten carried away. "It is half your own fault for being so irresistible," he said softly. "I can hardly believe your cousin had the temerity to suggest moving you into a lovenest. Why did he not have the wits to marry you?"

"He did not suggest a lovenest!" I gasped. "Where did you get such a idea?"

"You said he did not intend marriage."

"But he did not intend—that."

A frown creased Paton's brow. "What was all that about hiring a house? That has the ring of a man taking a mistress."

A spurt of anger invaded my happiness. "You would know all about that, of course!" I had intended to sound teasing, but the tinge of anger was evident.

"I never propositioned a *lady* at least!" he defended himself.

"You were within Ame's ace of it the day you took me to visit Angelina's cottage, and don't bother to deny it. If Lady DeGrue had not happened along . . ."

Paton gave a conscious, guilty start, but soon recovered. "So you *did* see through my little ruse. You are not as innocent as I thought. Odd you neglected to mention it."

"I saw no point in embarrassing us both."

"It was a misunderstanding. What was I to think when I found you amidst the rabble of Mrs. Speers's cohorts with some uncertainty as to your name? She had already hinted me in the direction of one of her tenants. I thought the place a sort of literary brothel."

"No doubt that is why you accepted her invitation!"

"She was writing a piece of fiction which she described to me as a biography of Madame de Staël. *That* is why I went, but it didn't take me long to get the aroma of the place."

"The aroma was familiar to you, I assume? If you did not like it, why did you linger?"

"To meet you."

"I didn't try to engage your interest."

He examined me with an insolent stare, and when he spoke, it was in his drawling, literary lecture voice. "Ladies have two modes of attracting a gentleman's attention. The first is by flirtation and insincere flattery. The second, used by more seasoned ladies, is to present a challenge. You seemed a past mistress of the latter sort."

"And you decided to egg me on by that patronizing lecture on literature!"

"Oh, no, that was to warn you off from expecting a review in the *Quarterly*. I keep business and pleasure separate when possible. I soon realized that you were a cut above the others at that rout. Why do you think I was so eager to get you out of here?"

"Into your own private brothel, you mean?"

"I am referring to Mr. Percival's flat. Not quite the mansion you and Miss Potter were so eager to boast of, but better than this." He gave a disgusted glance around the room. "I soon understood what you were trying to accomplish. To create a reputation for yourself in the literary world, by the shortcut of my infatuation. You had some strong words to say about Rousseau, but you have no more notion of his philosophy than I have of ladies' bonnets. That much was clear the day we drove to Corsham. However, I acquitted you of being a lightskirt."

"Generous of you!"

"I was happy to learn you were—respectable."

"A *lady*, Lord Paton, is the word you are looking for, or perhaps hesitate to confer on me."

"By God, you don't act like one! Why did you permit Nesbitt in the door after the way he has treated you?"

"He has treated me fairly. A good deal better than some!" I added with a blistering glare.

"Then why did you leave your home? It is inconceivable to me that a rational woman would flee from her home to live in a hovel, unless something was very much amiss. Why did you come to Bath? And having once chosen the most conventional, hidebound, gossip-ridden city in the kingdom, why did you proceed to flout every convention known to civilization? Why did you go to parties and balls when your father had just died? When I read your impassioned essay, I found it nearly possible to forgive you. I thought you had indeed been hard done by; now you calmly tell me your cousin, whom you libeled in your essay as 'a conspirator to the infamous practice of selling daughters,' has treated you fairly. Did it not occur to you to discuss your situation with him before taking off, to learn what precautions had been made in case you did not wish to marry him?"

Being revealed as a headstrong fool made me lose the last shred of my temper. "I don't have to explain my actions to you! I did what I thought best."

"You could hardly have done worse. Has he got some hold over you, Miss Nesbitt?" he asked in a last desperate attempt to explain the inexplicable.

"No. I was mistaken about Cousin Geoffrey. He came to clear up the misunderstanding."

"As it is apparently cleared up to your satisfaction, why does he return?"

"Other details remain to be ironed out. I must find a new place to live, and explain somehow why I have not been in mourning."

"If it is your intention to establish yourself as a decent woman in society, you will require a powerful iron."

"Bath isn't the only city in England. I can go somewhere else."

"People's tongues have a long reach, their pens even longer. This scandal will be known the length and breadth of the island before you're through. I don't know what is going on between you and your cousin, but it is not something I wish to be involved in. I regret I ever fell into your orbit."

"You don't regret it any more than I do! I don't need a sanctimonious hypocrite to read me lectures in propriety. You are a lecher, sir! You may have as many lightskirts as you please, but *I* am beyond the pale because I don't wear a black gown to mourn a father who hated me. It's ridiculous!"

"Ridiculous or not, it is the custom of our society. *The Ladies' Journal* may rant till the cows come home, it won't be changed in our lifetime. I shall tell Mr. Percival you won't be requiring the flat. Good evening, Miss Nesbitt. Pray give my best regards to Miss Potter."

He left, and I stood staring at the door, not know-ing whether I was more relieved to be rid of him, or sorry that I could not explain. After a thorough review of his various insults, I tried to view the situation objectively. My behavior must appear ir-rational to someone who had never been in the suds. What would Paton know of a lady's feelings upon her father's death, to find herself disinherited? He thought me either a fiend or a fool, and would in all probability warn his close friends to have nothing to do with me.

I had hoped that with his protection I might tell the whole truth and face down the quizzes of Bath, but without his friendship, it couldn't be done. I would return to Milverton with Geoffrey. Not to Nes-bitt Hall, but to some hired mansion in the vicinity, amidst all my old friends. My past was not sullied with any freakish behavior there. If rumors trickled back from Bath, they would take it for unfounded gossip, and accept me.

All this madness would be left behind, and with it all the fun and excitement. No more writing for *The Ladies' Journal,* no more visits from Paton or Isabel. No balls at the Upper or Lower Rooms, no tour of the Pump Room, no drives in the Crescent Gardens. My recent folly would be the scarlet secret in my past. Ladies had recovered from worse.

Annie heard the door close and returned, wearing a roguish grin. "Are congratulations in order?" she asked hopefully.

"Hardly. Paton thinks I am a Bedlamite."

"But he was on his knees, Emma! And with such a

look on his face, I made sure he was proposing. A man doesn't look like that if he is not in love."

"Or in hate. He despises me. I am beginning to sound like Lord Ronald."

"Did you tell him about your fortune?"

"Not specifically. I hinted at it."

"But what put him in a pucker, my dear?"

I leaned my head aback against the sofa. "Everything. I begin to think continuing here at Bath is impossible. Would you mind very much if we returned home, Annie? Or are you and Arthur . . ."

She blushed and simpered. "He hasn't asked me. The threat of leaving might very well turn the trick."

"I shan't urge you to refuse if you really care for him. I'll go home alone."

"Oh, Emma! You make me feel like a beast. Not that you would miss me once you got back to Milverton! Mrs. Stacey would be happy to act as your companion. In any case, you cannot leave till Geoffrey has a crack at Miss Bonham. There is no hurry to leave Bath. You can sulk in your room as well here as there."

I had expected more sympathy from Annie. Love had turned her into a monster of selfishness, to go telling me the truth. Annie carried the clean glasses, and I poured more wine. Would I turn into a gin drinker, like Mrs. Speers, as old age and disillusionment came upon me? Perhaps I should buy a rooming house and enlarge my fortune. But all I felt up to was crawling into my bed and pulling the covers over my head, which is what I did.

Paton had come this evening to proclaim his love. He had kissed me madly, and told me none of it was my fault. And I had reveled in those brief moments of glory. How had I turned his mission into a débâcle? Where had I gone wrong? Should I have let him believe Geoffrey was a scoundrel, and he a knight to rescue me from perdition? Obviously that was unjust to my cousin. Did Paton expect me to apologize and grovel while he called me a conniver and a user and an ignoramus? I never claimed to be a scholar of Rousseau's infamous philosophy. I never tried to conceal that I wished to get a review in his magazine. I did not try to engage his interest by some cunning trick, as he imagined.

Paton was in the wrong as much as I. He was a lecher, and I loved him so much that my whole body ached.

Chapter Fifteen

My major activities over the next few days were harping on Paton's last, calamitous visit and fashioning a dowdy black gown from a bolt of bombazine purchased by Annie. The tedium of this job was interrupted upon occasion by various minor irritations in the form of visits from Mrs. Speers and Mr. Bellows. Geoffrey called often, usually alone but twice with Isabel. I could not go on being ill with an unidentified malady forever, so I was now officially in mourning for the death of an unspecified cousin, who had left me a small fortune. That much unsteady groundwork was laid for my rehabilitation.

I saw that Geoffrey was falling into the abyss of love. He looked like a moonling when Isabel spoke. His eyes lingered on her, and his lips were perpetually lifted in a witless half smile. He was scarcely aware of anyone else's presence when she was with him. No such reciprocal tokens of lunacy adorned Isabel's visage. She treated him not quite like a dog, but like a hired companion. It was taken for granted he would do as he was bid, which was about the worst mistake he could make. He had not convinced her he was a dashing rake. I dare say it was impossible, when he had simultaneously to fulfill Lady DeGrue's notions of a proper suitor.

I took him to task for it one morning when he dropped in without her. "I can't be savage with her. She is too sweet" was his excuse.

"Anyone would be sweet when she is never crossed. Try refusing her something, and see how sweet she is."

He said he would try, in a doubtful way that did not promise much success.

"Does she ever speak of Lord Ronald?" I inquired.

"Not a word. I believe she has forgotten him. She seems perfectly content to have her escorts limited to myself."

No lady who is just discovering her powers with the opposite sex would be content with so little. She liked Geoffrey; she did not love him. That satisfied glow on her pretty face had a different cause, and I felt an alarming fear that it was Lord Ronald.

"Do you ever bump into Lord Ronald when you are driving out with Isabel?" I inquired.

"Bath is a small city. We see him about, here and there, but they are never alone. He knows Isabel likes the Crescent Gardens, and walks there to catch a glimpse of her, I suppose. I cannot help feeling sorry for the young bleater, but I never let her out of my sight."

"Drive her somewhere else, Geoffrey," Annie suggested. "He is probably slipping her notes or some such thing."

Geoffrey stiffened up and informed us that Isabel was not that kind of girl. He would not listen to a word against Isabel, and Isabel would not hear a word against Lord Ronald, for I still hammered at her whenever I got the chance. It seemed all our advice was falling on deaf ears, till Geoffrey returned that evening around nine.

He came storming in with a face like a thundercloud and said, "I hope you are satisfied, Cousin. You have driven us apart."

"What happened?" Annie demanded.

"I did as Emma suggested, and insisted on driving Isabel to the Sydney Gardens today instead of the Crescent. Now she is angry with me. She told me that if my only intention is to vex her, I need not call this evening. I called anyhow, for Lady DeGrue expected me to. Isabel sent down word that she had a fit of the megrims. Tomorrow I shall drive her to Crescent Gardens," he added firmly.

"It is not the trees and bushes that hold such a strong fascination at the Crescent Gardens," I pointed out.

"No, it is that jackanapes of an Etherington lurking behind them that draws her there," Annie agreed.

Geoffrey was beginning to admit we were right. "Well, he did not get a glimpse of her today," he retorted.

He stayed longer than usual, as he wanted an audience for his tale of unrequited love. It was a theme of some interest to me, and I soon became his sole auditor. Annie got a reprieve in the person of Arthur Pepper, who came to call only slightly less often than Geoffrey. No announcement had been made, but an agreement was certainly simmering between them. Did I think to mention that Arthur took Mr. Percival's rooms in the Westgate Buildings and took Annie to approve them? His removing from the wrong side of the river was considered as a preliminary to the proposal of marriage.

Arthur took his leave around ten-thirty. We were just hinting Geoffrey away when flying footsteps were heard on the staircase. For some foolish reason I thought of Lord Paton, perhaps because he and Geoffrey had twice passed on the stairs. I could not imagine what was happening when I opened the door to one of Lady DeGrue's liveried footmen, who carried a note in his hand.

"Is Mr. Nesbitt here, ma'am?" he asked, looking over my shoulder to Geoffrey.

Geoffrey dashed forward and snatched the note. "When you wasn't at the Pelican, I figured you might be with your cousin," the footman said. He watched with an eager face as Geoffrey read the note. Annie and I wore the same expression.

"She's gone!" Geoffrey exclaimed. His face turned bone-white and his eyes seemed to grow black. The paper trembled in his fingers.

Annie demanded "Who?" and I asked "Isabel?" at the same moment.

The footman could no longer contain his excitement. "Packed up a pair of bandboxes and slipped out the liberry door. It wasn't out her bedroom winder, for there was no ladder."

"When? How long ago?" Geoffrey shouted.

"There'd be no way of knowing, would there?" was the footman's unsatisfactory reply. "She ate her dinner at seven, and said she had a megrim. The old dame went to say good night at ten, and found a piller stuffed under the covers. She was very nearly conned, but she wanted to check the young lady for a fever, and that's how she found Miss Bonham had tipped her the double."

"This is Etherington's work. I must go to Lady DeGrue at once," Geoffrey said, and headed for the door without even picking up his curled beaver.

"The ladies are wanted as well, if you'll have a look at the note," the footman said. "For propriety's sake. We wouldn't want Miss Bonham to spend the night with just two bachelors. 'Twould be almost worse than one."

"Quite right," Geoffrey said distractedly. "Get your bonnet, Emma."

I was already flying to my bedchamber, Annie a step behind me. "I knew this would happen," I said in exasperation. "I wonder how much of a lead they have."

"And where they could be heading," Annie added.

"It would be Gretna Green. Until he marries her, he cannot get his filthy paws on her money."

We bolted downstairs at a great pace, discussing the matter as we went. "I think we ought to head straight for Gretna Green and let Annie go over to comfort Lady DeGrue," I suggested to Geoffrey. "We don't want Etherington to get any farther ahead than he already has."

"Lady DeGrue might have something to help us— she might have found a note," he parried.

Mrs. Speers came staggering out of the saloon, reeking of gin. "Is something amiss, Miss Nisbitt?" she asked.

"Nothing, thank you. We can't stop to chat now."

We piled into Geoffrey's carriage and bowled along to Quiet Street. Lady DeGrue looked like death. She was wringing her hands and pacing to and fro in the gloomy old Gold Saloon, blaming herself for everything.

"I should have gone up to her sooner. It is all my fault. I left the poor child alone with a migraine."

I put an arm around her poor bony shoulders and made her sit on the sofa. "Don't blame yourself," I said. "Annie, get some wine for Lady DeGrue." If blame belonged on anyone but the culprits, it was on me. I was the one who had unwittingly loosened Isabel's chains. I knew in my heart she would never have done such a thing before I convinced her she was treated like a child. The trouble was that she *was* a child, insofar as practical worldly knowledge went. Lord Ronald would not have given her a second look if I had not talked her into the dashing high poke bonnet, for that matter.

"She didn't leave a note?" Geoffrey asked.

"No, not a word." Poor Lady DeGrue tried to stand up, and fell back on the sofa. "We must be off at once," she said.

"You are not going anywhere. Miss Potter and I shall go with Geoffrey," I told her firmly.

She looked at me with the eyes of a whipped dog and said in a low voice, "What will Mr. Nesbitt think of her? He will never offer for her now. Such an excellent parti."

"Hush. He loves her better than that, Lady DeGrue. We shall bring her back, and see them married before any scandal breaks."

She patted my hand. "You were always so kind to Isabel. I wish there were some way I could repay you, Miss Nesbitt."

The others joined us for a hurried discussion of

Isabel's recovery. Geoffrey drew out his watch. "If they left around eight—and they could not have left much earlier—they would have gone about . . ." He frowned. "In Lord Ronald's carriage, and with that team of grays, I shall never overtake them."

"Geoffrey!" I scolded, for this speech threw Lady DeGrue into another spasm of trembling. "We don't know when they left. Perhaps it was only minutes before Lady DeGrue discovered her gone. We'll hire a better team."

"Her bed was cold," Lady DeGrue said with a forlorn shake of her head.

"What we really require is a curricle," Geoffrey decided. "It would make twice the time, but mine is at home, and of course the livery stable at Bath has none for hire."

Lady DeGrue looked up from her handkerchief. "Lord Paton, Miss Nesbitt," she said hopefully. "He has the best bloods in all of Bath. We shan't mind his knowing about this disaster, as he is such a close friend of yours. And his discretion can be counted on."

The idea filled me with horror. How could I ask the help of a man who despised me? I had no claim on Paton's charity. Besides, I had not heard from him for two days, and had no idea where he was. I thought he might even have returned to London by now. "I'm afraid I don't know where he is this evening," I said.

It was true, but it was also true that he had the best nags in Bath. If anyone could overtake Lord Ronald, it was surely Paton. But we could not afford to waste time trying to locate him. It seemed hard to leave Lady DeGrue alone, and I added, "Annie, do you think you might stay . . ."

"She should not be alone," Annie agreed. "You two run along. I'm too old to be battering along in the dark of night."

Geoffrey and I ran back to the waiting carriage.

"I wonder if they are really headed to Scotland," I said.

"It's certainly marriage he has in mind, but Gretna Green is a mighty long haul. It would take days to reach it from Bath, and he knows Isabel is not without friends."

"Perhaps he'll try for something closer," I worried.

"London is a mighty long haul too. His father's estate is nearly as far away, in Cornwall. The man has no imagination. It'll be Gretna Green. At least he cannot marry her till he gets her there. We'll overtake him long before that."

"He doesn't have to marry her. Once he spends the night with her, she'll have no choice but to have him."

I had spoken without thinking, and I could see how my words affected Geoffrey. He froze into a perfect statue, with his lips clenched tightly together. "I'll kill the scoundrel," he growled. Something in his voice reminded me of a mad dog.

He urged the coachman to go faster, till we were flying along the road, being mercilessly tossed to and fro in the carriage.

"Do you think we should stop and make inquiries at some of the inns?" I suggested.

"Not yet. There's no point till we get a few hours from Bath. He won't risk being seen and recognized close to home. By Stroud, or thereabouts, he'll start to feel safe."

Our destination was a little more than twenty-five miles, when the twisting road was taken into account. There was no escaping hills. Our trip took us into Cotswold country, through pretty villages with magnificent churches. The hunting boxes of the wealthy stood atop the hills and nestled into the valleys beyond. With relentless pressure on John Groom and the nags, we made it to Stroud in three hours, with a few stops at inns close to the city. The town was as hard on the horses as Bath. It rests on the steep side of a narrow valley, with the Thames and Severn cutting through it.

It was the dead of night, actually early morning, for it was after two o'clock when we arrived. There was no gaslight in this part of the country. The buildings were all dark except the inns, where torches blazed outside and a few lights within told us some-one was still up.

"Where shall we begin?" Geoffrey asked, his eye running down the main street to three or four establishments.

"Right here, at the Three Feathers."

I was cramped and sore and tired. My eyes felt as if someone had thrown sand in them, and I was as hungry as a horse. But it was a relief to have reached Stroud, and I alit from the carriage with hope soaring. We went into the Three Feathers and straight to the desk, where Geoffrey roused the clerk by ringing the desk bell. Within two minutes we knew Isabel was not here. The performance was repeated at the Rose and Thistle, the George, and the Shipwalk, with the same results.

We returned to the carriage, crestfallen. "We must make a tour of all the inns close by, just beyond town," I said. "Etherington is poor. Perhaps they are putting up at a smaller, cheaper establishment."

"Or rushing straight on to Gretna Green," Geoffrey said, jaw muscles working.

"They are only made of flesh and bone, like us. They will have stopped somewhere nearby. They are at some inn, having dinner and taking a rest."

Geoffrey's jaws clenched furiously. "I'll kill him," he growled in a very good parody of a hero. Unfortunately he had brought neither pistol nor sword with him, and I did not think him capable of execution with his bare hands.

"Let us continue and try the next spot," I suggested.

We re-entered the carriage and went on to a small stone place called Jack Duck's Tavern, with a discreet sign in the window saying Rooms, Meals, Ale. "He wouldn't have brought her here," Geoffrey said, nose turning down.

"It's worth a try. In any case, the front hall is all lit up inside. We shan't have to rouse the clerk. Geoffrey! Maybe Etherington has already done it for us! Why is this place ablaze when none of the others were? They've had a recent arrival!"

"By God, you could be right! I'll nip around to the stable before we enter and see if his carriage is here." He left, to return a moment later, bristling with success. "They're here! And he cannot have had time to—I mean they only arrived fifteen minutes ago."

"Let us go in!"

Chapter Sixteen

A DECREPIT OLD hag wrapped in mismatched and soiled shawls sat at the desk thumbing through a copy of *The Ladies' Journal*. Was this really my audience! Before we said a word she turned a knowing, bloodshot eye on us. "Too late, dearies. I'm all filled up. If you'd care to wait an hour, Mr. Smith may be finished with his suite. He must get his lady home before morning."

"Good God!" Geoffrey exclaimed, and looked at me as if he would like to cover my ears. "You'd best wait in the carriage, Emma. This is no place for a lady."

It was a temptation, but before I decided, the air was pierced with a shriek, coming from behind a door across the hallway. Geoffrey and I exchanged a look of mute horror. "Isabel!" we said in unison, and darted to the door. It was locked. The hag waggled her head and said, "Mr. Jones is a bit of a lad, but he never hurts them."

"Open this door at once!" I demanded.

Geoffrey was already slamming at it, first with his shoulder, and next with his foot, which proved more effective. The battered old door flew open and we stared at just such a lively scene of dissipation as we had both been dreading for three hours. A flushed and disheveled Lord Ronald was trying vainly to pull Isabel into his arms. His dainty coiffure was all askew. He had flung off his kerchief and opened his shirt halfway to his waist. There wasn't a hair to be seen on his white but well-muscled chest. The glazed appearance of his eyes and the empty bottle of wine bore testimony to his condition.

Isabel looked even worse. Her gown, though in no danger of being ripped from her body, was totally destroyed, with mud splashes all over the skirt. Her face was grimed, and she was fighting off Etherington's advances. When she saw us, her face screwed up into a knot and tears spurted out.

"Geoffrey!" she bawled, and went running into his arms, where she cried herself to a pulp.

"Now, see here!" Lord Ronald blustered, but in a slurred voice.

Geoffrey set Isabel aside into my keeping and turned the wrath of Jehovah on the villain. "You will answer for this, sir!"

"This is none of your affair," Etherington said.

Isabel clutched on to my arm. "Oh, he's going to challenge Ronald to a duel. Do you think he'll kill him?"

It was soon clear that a duel was not what Geoffrey had in mind. He raised his fists and laid Etherington flat with one well-aimed blow at his handsome nose. Etherington subsided gracefully onto the sofa. Blood did not spurt from the nose, but it oozed in an ugly dark dribble. Geoffrey pulled him up by the collar and went at him again.

I used the time to quiz Isabel. "Did he do anything?" I demanded. I did not refer to her muddied and frazzled state, of course, but to her intrinsic virtue.

She understood perfectly. A fierce light glowed in her eye, and she said, "No, but he meant to, and before we were married! You were right about him, Emma. I was never so taken in in my whole life. He didn't even have a wedding ring for me!"

The second blow either knocked Etherington unconscious, or showed him the wisdom of pretending it had. He lay prostrate on the floor, motionless.

"Get him out of here," I said.

The harridan appeared at the doorway. "Friends of the young lady, are you? Shall I have it removed?" she asked, nudging at Etherington's carcass with the toe of her shoe.

"If you please," I said.

She whistled down the hall, and two stout ruffians came bounding in. "Put Mr. Jones to bed," she ordered them, and left, carrying his curled beaver and coat. I noticed her fingers sliding into the coat pockets, but could not have cared less.

Geoffrey cast one frustrated look on Isabel, trying to decide whether to ring a peal over her, or crush her into his arms as he wanted to. She decided the matter for him by rushing into his arms and claiming him as her hero. He had little recourse then but to pat her on the back and comfort her, while she, sobbing and gasping, poured out her story. This, then, was how I ought to have behaved with Paton. Fancy Isabel being so wise, when she had not a particle of common sense or actual experience.

Sensing it was to be a long story, I asked the harridan to bring us wine, and we all found seats. I left the sofa to the lovers and made do with an uncomfortable, hard chair. Isabel held center stage, and was crafty enough to heap abuse on herself before we could do it. E'er long Geoffrey was persuaded she was fortunate to have survived her ordeal at all. He clung to her hands as if she might vanish before his very eyes.

"I have been so foolish," she said, casting sheep's eyes on Geoffrey. "But he told me we would be married immediately. I thought he had got a license, for I am over twenty-one, you know. He was supposed to have a minister here, waiting for us. But he didn't have one, or even a wedding ring."

"How did you get so dirty?" I asked.

"He brought me in an open carriage," she said, fire sparking from her eyes. "In case anyone recognized his own, he said, but I learned later he had to give it to someone called Quincy to cover a bet, and all he could borrow was a curricle. So we had to drive in a freezing rig. He brought a bottle of brandy to keep *himself* warm, but what of *me*? Then we lost a wheel outside of town, for the roads are a disgrace. Ronald despises manual work, so *I* had to run down the hill after it myself in my best slippers. He wanted to sleep under the starry sky, by a rippling brook. Only there were no stars, and besides, he didn't even bring a blanket! He used my money to get the wheel fixed, and once we got here, he didn't order a thing to eat, only wine."

"The bounder!" Geoffrey said, clasping her hands tightly.

I swallowed my smile and urged her on to tell all. That she hadn't had a bite since leaving home featured as large as the real outrages. The runaway had been engineered wholly by the ineffectual Etherington, by means of notes smuggled to her in the park. He left them in a bush, she rescued them while pretending to admire the foliage, and left off a reply the next day. When Geoffrey refused to take her to the park, Lord Ronald risked throwing pebbles at her window, and they agreed to flee that very night.

"We were to be married here, and go on to London," she explained. "And I am glad now the minister wasn't here, for I have come to see Lord Ronald is very selfish. Why, I wouldn't be a bit surprised if it was only my money he was after. He certainly took no pains for my comfort."

I did not hesitate to utter the dread words, "I told you so." Geoffrey was all sweetness and understanding. Isabel was all contrition, and we were eager to get away.

"But first we must eat something," she decreed.

"Not here, Isabel," I said. "Let us go to one of the better inns. The food in this place will be even worse than the wine, and this drink tastes like paint thinner."

"Is there someplace you can clean up?" Geoffrey asked her.

There were no facilities in the parlor for making a toilette. The hag showed Isabel to a little cubbyhole with a dingy mirror and a grimy washbasin. I was going to help her, but there was hardly room for one, so I said, "Just wash your face and brush your hair. Your pelisse will cover the state of your gown." Then I returned to Geoffrey to discuss the matter.

"You'd best have a word with Etherington, warning him not to mention this affair," I suggested.

"Yes, I will before we leave. Should I challenge him to a duel?" he asked doubtfully.

"Don't be such a clothhead, Geoffrey. What good would that do?"

"But if her reputation is ruined . . ."

"Then you'll just have to marry her." I smiled.

He looked as if I had conferred a title on him. "Do you think she'll have me?"

"I shouldn't be surprised. I believe she's learned her lesson now."

"I'll see Etherington at once, and we can leave as soon as Isabel returns."

He left, and I poured myself another glass of the paint thinner, which was slightly better than nothing. I was just sipping my wine when the door of the inn burst open and flying footsteps were heard in the hallway. The old hag spoke. "We don't supply girls. You have to bring your own," she informed the customer. Apparently the place was a well-known den of iniquity.

"I'm not here for sex. I've come to commit murder," a man's voice growled. I hardly recognized Lord Paton's usually polite accents, but the timbre of the voice was familiar.

"Don't do it in here," the hag said sharply. "I don't want the constable sniffing around. Take him down to the river. That's a fine place for it. You can throw the corpse in the water and no one will be any the wiser."

Lady DeGrue must have been in touch with Paton, and he'd come to help. I hastened to the doorway. He was just turning from the desk. He saw me, and I watched in astonishment as his face congealed to white ice. I had thought he'd be happy to see he had caught up with us. But of course he had no way of knowing we had rescued Isabel. He was still worried about her, but it was not worry that distorted his features so. It was hatred.

"In here, Paton," I called, trying to behave as normally as the conditions permitted.

He advanced at a stiff stride, as though his knees had turned to wood. His eyes were like burning coals in his white face. Lines were etched deeply from his nose to the edge of his lips, and the lips were thin.

"Are you sure it isn't a case of three being a crowd?" he asked ironically. Those burning eyes never left mine. Why was he behaving so weirdly? Apparently he saw I was alone without looking at the rest of the room, for he asked, "Where's Nesbitt?"

"Just taking care of a little necessary business so we can leave immediately. How did you find us?"

"I was told Gretna Green was the destination. It seemed an illogical choice to me, but that's what the lady said."

"Why did you find it odd?"

The blood returned to his face all in a tide, till he was nearly the color of a beet. "You've reached the age of consent. You don't have to indulge in a runaway match, to have the nuptials performed over the anvil. He has no intention of marrying you, or he'd have done it in Bath, or Milverton." This was delivered in an angry rush.

"I am not getting married!" I stood, dumbfounded. *I* had reached the age of consent. He thought *I* was the runaway—and Mr. Nesbitt my bridegroom! Before I could recover sufficiently to correct him, he lashed out at me again.

"Then the more fool you! If you are to be had for a carte blanche, you would have found me a more pleasing and generous protector."

Protector! So it was only a mistress-ship that occurred to him. A memory of Isabel's tears and accusations came to me, only to be rejected. The sane course would be to correct Paton at once, but I felt a strong urge to hear him go his length. I would use no inferior, feminine wiles to beguile him.

My voice was cold as crystal, and I donned a chilly, uncaring smile. "You have a high opinion of your charms, sir! Neither that shack in the wilds nor a second-hand pair of cream ponies tempted me in the least. As to the charms of your person, I'd sooner live with a hottentot."

A flame leapt in his eyes. "You seemed eager enough to drive out with me in the beginning!"

"Yes, indeed, for as you so cleverly surmised, you had one thing that interested me. All I ever wanted from you was a favorable review in your magazine, and I made no effort to conceal the fact. I wanted that very much, but not enough to have you into the bargain. That lofty journal, of course, is reserved for scholarly gentlemen like Coleridge, who enlighten the world with their dream ravings of magic castles and dead albatrosses. Nor could I hope to compete with such monsters of dissipation as Lord Byron. I am neither foolish nor lecherous enough to merit your literary attention. Whatever induced you to imagine I was interested in any *other* sort of attention I cannot conceive."

"We reviewed Hannah More too!"

"That sanctimonious old spinster was careful not to tamper with your prejudices, and supported your theory that women's place is in the home, mending your socks!"

"You were eager enough for my friendship, even after the farce of . . ."

"I should have thought a heavy reader like yourself knows Hope springs eternal in the human breast, milord. While there was a chance you realized a piece of writing ought not to be judged by its cover, but actually read and considered, I continued to see you."

He stiffened up even straighter. "And I would have thought a young lady who is so intimately aware of man's base, rapacious nature and society's conventions would know more than to jeopardize her reputation by such behavior as this. This is even worse than the manner in which you celebrated your father's passing."

"It's none of your affair what I do!"

His nostrils dilated, and his loud voice lowered a notch. "No, but it was when I made the error of haring off after you. I had intended to marry you, you see, in spite of all your self-imposed ineligibility."

It was all I could do to keep from slapping him. It was not a proposal, but even a *mention* of a proposal ought not to be delivered in such an arrogant, self-consequential way, as though he were offering a crown, or a ticket to heaven.

"A pity you hadn't mentioned it to me sooner, and you would have saved yourself the trip. Marriage to anyone, and most particularly to you, is not a part of my plans."

He stared so hard, I felt he was looking inside my head. Frustration and impatience and anger were all mixed up in that look. "What, exactly, is your plan, Miss Nesbitt? I see no pattern in your behavior, no sane plot, but only the folly of a misguided woman reeling giddily, till she finally succeeds in throwing herself off a cliff."

"My plot, obviously too convoluted for you to grasp, is to return Isabel to her aunt before anyone discovers she ran off with Lord Ronald. *That* is why Mr. Nesbitt and I are here."

He looked ready to contradict me, but before I had the pleasure of further discommoding him, Geoffrey and Isabel appeared at the doorway. She wore the chastened air of the lamb gone astray, and Geoffrey the undeniable face of the saviour. Lord Paton was speechless. To forestall his blurting out something to reveal our conversation, I hastened into speech.

I fixed Paton with an imperious eye and announced, "Lord Paton came to help us."

Paton looked relieved. Geoffrey was loud in his thanks, Isabel more muted in her apologies. I said not a word, but enjoyed the little entr'acte immensely. Geoffrey mentioned that Lady DeGrue had suggested asking for Paton's assistance, and Paton did not deny that she had done so.

"I'm sorry I could not have been of some real assistance," he said.

Geoffrey, trying to butter up the nobleman, made a complete jackass of himself. "You were a great help, Lord Paton. We couldn't have done it without you. I'm sure I speak for Isabel and Emma as well when I tell you how delighted we are that you're here."

"But you must not tell anyone!" Isabel cautioned.

Geoffrey gave her a chiding look. "I don't think you need deliver Lord Paton a lesson in chivalry, my dear. He would never do anything to embarrass a lady."

I gave Paton a cool look. "No indeed. I'm sure he has *read* all about chivalry, and is eager for a chance to put his knowledge into practice. Shall we go?"

"Isabel wants to have a bite before we begin the trip home," Geoffrey said. "Where would you suggest, Lord Paton?"

They settled on the George, where Paton was invited (by Geoffrey) to join us. I was amazed that he accepted. In his position I would rather have driven without food to the edge of the world. Over our meal, Isabel had a second chance to tell of her night's horrors, and Geoffrey to play the stern but loving moral guide. Paton and I took the opportunity of pretending we were not aware of each other's presence at the table. The gentlemen had a private word while they were settling the bill, and I gave Isabel a Bear Garden jaw about hurting Lady DeGrue.

As we went toward the carriages, Geoffrey said, "You're driving back with Paton, Emma. I've spoken to him. I mean to propose to Isabel on the way home. I ought really to speak to Lady DeGrue first, but under the circumstances, Lord Paton thinks it will not be considered ill bred, as she has shown a marked approval of me."

"She'll be tickled pink, Geoffrey. In a way, I've already spoken to her. I suggested something of the sort, and she was thrilled."

"Really! I shall ask Paton to stand as witness for the nuptials."

He was quite as arrogant as Paton in assuming a positive reply. Paton approached me and said, "Mr. Nesbitt told you of the driving arrangements?"

"Yes."

"Luckily I knew the trip would be a long one, and drove my carriage and team of four. My groom has got us a fresh team for the drive back."

"Good."

He handed me into the carriage. I settled into a corner with a rug over my knees, closed my eyes, and pretended to be asleep. Sleep was the farthest thing from my mind, but it was my intention to stay that way till the carriage drew up to Lampards Street. Behind my closed lids there swarmed such a varied array of scenes, it reminded me of Brewster's new toy, the kaleidoscope, with people taking the place of colored glass chips.

Papa was there, and Geoffrey, with Nesbitt Hall hulking in the background. No longer my home, but a place I would visit Isabel and Geoffrey, after their marriage. I would have friends to visit in Bath as well, as Annie and Pepper would settle here, in Mr. Percival's flat. I never did meet Mr. Percival. Perhaps I would call on Mrs. Speers, and deliver her a copy of my gothic novel, after it became a huge success. And of course I must visit Lady DeGrue.

I realized that in this human kaleidoscope, I was the unsettled piece. I would be visiting everyone, but from where? Where would I live? The darkest piece in the set was Lord Paton, and I put off thinking of him till the last. I would not be able to hold my tongue once I started reviewing my grievances and a three-hour argument was more than I was up to. For half an hour the horses clip-clopped hypnotically through the night. My bones became weary and I shifted to relieve the pressure.

"Warm enough?" Paton asked the moment I stirred. His voice, fully alert, told me he had not been resting.

"Yes, thank you," I murmured drowsily.

"Since you are awake, Miss Nesbitt . . ."

I made a sleepy "Mmmm" sound, designed to discourage conversation.

He ignored it and said, "I want to apologize for what I said at Stroud. I thought you and Nesbitt . . . The thing is, you see, I went to Lampards Street to call on you this evening. Mrs. Speers said you and Nesbitt had gone bolting out of the house. She overheard you urging him to go to Gretna Green. She thought he put up some argument. It was my intention to rescue you."

"You should not have paid any attention to my landlady. She's always bosky by evening."

"She was, but I had her call the servant, and she corroborated it."

I gave off all pretence of being sleepy. "Did they not tell you Miss Potter was with us?"

"No! I don't know—I was in such a state, I wasn't hearing too clearly, but I do remember now that she wasn't in your flat when I broke down the—when I—entered."

"You broke our door!"

"Just the lock!" he assured me. "I'll have it fixed."

"Everyone in the house will have been in our rooms by now, pawing through our belongings," I scolded him. "Why can't you mind your own business? And why were you there anyway?"

"I wanted to see you, to continue discussing rationally what we began to speak of last night."

I listened with interest. "You already had the fool-

200

ish idea that Geoffrey was trying to bullox me into—"

He cut me off sharply. "I don't mean that! You wanted to iron out the difficulties of your position. I gave it considerable thought, after I left you, and I think you should brazen it out. There is no point pretending your father has been dead a year. Once a young lady inherits a fortune, people suddenly take a keen interest in her origins. Someone will discover he died just weeks before you attacked the Upper Rooms."

"I did not attack them! I attended! Why do you always make me sound a wretch?"

"It was an attack on convention. You should have been in deep mourning. You thought your father had disinherited you, and in retaliation you went on a spree. I think people can understand, and forgive that. I did, when I read your essay, and so did Lady Forrest."

"You *told* her!" My voice was thin and cutting, like a scalpel.

"On the understanding that she was not to repeat it. I wanted an older and wiser person's opinion. My aunt thinks it will be a nine day's wonder, like Willie Kemp's dance from London to Norwich. Lady DeGrue will make her crew toe the line. She has her own secret, which we are privy to. The greatest problem is that you would have to go into mourning, now that the will is straightened out."

"I intend to. Why do you think I'm wearing this hideous black gown?"

"I thought it was very becoming."

"I look like a witch, and if you think to beguile

me with that sort of meaningless compliment, I suggest you stop and let me get back to sleep."

"You weren't sleeping. You were as stiff as a board, and your hands were moving the whole time," he said sharply. But when he resumed, his tone was softer. "Emma, we have to talk, and we aren't likely to have a better opportunity than this. I admit my first intention toward you did not include marriage. What was I to think, meeting you as I did? I only knew that you were beautiful and intelligent, and I wanted to see a good deal more of you." His hand moved across the space and gripped mine.

"And like a true gentleman, you turned off your mistress," I reminded him.

"I planned to be faithful to my mistress at least. When I learned you were not a—what I—"

"A lightskirt."

"Ahem. Yes, I soon realized I still wanted you—for my wife. I still do, Emma." His body followed his arm across the space, and he sat beside me.

"You had an odd way of showing it!"

His arm stole around my waist, drawing me into his arms. "You called me a lecher."

"You *are* a lecher."

His breaths invaded my ear, causing a peculiar and highly enjoyable sensation of insanity. "But a faithful lecher who loves you very much." A trail of kisses glided along my chin, leaving fire and tingles in their wake.

I heard light, uneven breaths echo in the carriage, and realized they were my own. My heart pounded with rapid, fierce beats, like a hare's in chase. "A honeymoon, say in Italy and France, would solve the problem of mourning. No one would be observing what you wore, or where you went," he said softly.

"I don't intend to dishonor my father's memory by gallivanting."

"All the better. I'll have you to myself."

His lips found mine, and burned a kiss that was like a brand, marking and sealing me for life. "I can't get married when I'm in mourning—can I?" I asked weakly.

"Geoffrey plans to. A quiet do, with just family in attendance, and a brief announcement in the papers. If there is a little talk, we shan't hear it. And when we return, we'll be living in London, where there will be greater scandals than ours to titillate society."

"London? I should like to meet some other writers!"

He traced my chin with his thumb. "You haven't given me your answer, Emma. Must I resort to bribery—a review in the *Quarterly*? We don't usually review question marks, but—"

"But for a question mark with a coronet on top, you might make an exception?"

"Providing it is *my* coronet!"

"I suspected all along you could do it if you wanted to. You said you had no say in the matter."

"I didn't realize that was my sole attraction at the time. Now I am coming to know you better," he said, but with a teasing smile that still bordered on the arrogant.

"Just so you don't expect me to buy a pig in poke. First I'll read my review, *then* I shall decide whether I shall have you."

"Emma! It's all decided."

"Is it, Paton? You must convince me of it."

Like any overbearing man, he tried to convince me by amorous physical violence, and like any ninnyhammer in love, I let him succeed. But I shall still get my review, I promise you! And I shall continue to fight any French philosophy that I see being perpetrated around me as well.

Many hours later, when Isabel was safely returned and the rest of us met at Lampards Street, Geoffrey announced that he would be married within the week, and take his bride to Nesbitt Hall immediately afterward. Paton and I were to be married at his father's estate. He assured me the duke would be so happy to see him settle down he would not mind that the bride wore black.

That evening I re-read my diary, and was amazed at how angry it sounded. I am no Boadicea, nor do I much admire her. I looked her up at the circulating library, and believe she would have done better to bat her eyes at the governor Suetonius and conciliate him, rather than massacre seventy thousand Romans and Britons. There is more than one way to skin a cat. Rome regained what she had captured in any case, Boadicea took poison, and thousands more were killed in the ensuing warfare. She was apparently unaware of the old Roman adage, Love Conquers All.